D1345051

1149031

HAUNTED BY THE PAST

One morning, Rose Murray's life is shattered by a ghost from the past — a 'phone call from Alex Sutton. In her teens she had been infatuated with Alex, although he was a tearaway. Rose has been happily married to Tom, the village doctor, for four years and they have a three-year-old daughter. Now Alex, out of prison, wants to see her for old times' sake. But when they meet, feelings which had lain buried begin to surface . . .

Books by Judy Chard
in the Linford Romance Library:

PERSON UNKNOWN
TO BE SO LOVED
ENCHANTMENT
APPOINTMENT WITH DANGER
BETRAYED
THE SURVIVORS
TO LIVE WITH FEAR
SWEET LOVE REMEMBERED
WINGS OF THE MORNING
A TIME TO LOVE
THE UNCERTAIN HEART
THE OTHER SIDE OF SORROW
THE WEEPING AND THE LAUGHTER
THROUGH THE GREEN WOODS
RENDEZVOUS WITH LOVE
SEVEN LONELY YEARS

JUDY CHARD

HAUNTED BY THE PAST

Complete and Unabridged

LINFORD
Leicester

First published in Great Britain in 1982

First Linford Edition
published 2004

British Library CIP Data

Chard, Judy
  Haunted by the pas
  Large print ed.—
  Linford romance lit
  1. Love stories
  2. Large type books
  I. Title
  823.9′14 [F]

ISBN 1–84395–562–8

Published by
F. A. Thorpe (Publishing)
Anstey, Leicestershire

Set by Words & Graphics Ltd.
Anstey, Leicestershire
Printed and bound in Great Britain by
T. J. International Ltd., Padstow, Cornwall

This book is printed on acid-free paper

1

Rose sat for a moment in front of her dressing table mirror — she didn't often have time to spend on her appearance, although it was not exactly neglected — but this morning for some reason she felt as if she had reached some kind of crossroads in her life. Perhaps it was because of the letter Tom had had yesterday offering him the chance of a job at the big London teaching hospital where he'd done his training.

'Darling, they want to see me,' he had said, looking up at her over the breakfast table. 'They like the letter I wrote and they've checked with old Harrison; he put in a good word for his ex-student! I think there's a real chance we may get to London, be where it's all happening in the medical world as well as on all the other scenes

— as the young have it.'

She had tried to be enthusiastic, to encourage, but she had suddenly felt cold; the thought of returning to London and the accompanying circumstances had made a cloud which had darkened her day. She had slept badly, too. Tom had been on call but they had had a quiet night as far as the phone was concerned. This morning, however, the mirror reflected dark shadows under her eyes — she hoped Tom wouldn't notice. In spite of his being a doctor he didn't really seem to notice when she or Sharon were off colour, she supposed it was like the old adage of the cobbler having no shoes.

The mirror reflected a high cheekboned face, blue eyes and corn coloured hair worn in a smooth sweep to her shoulders — a powdering of freckles across her nose — an older edition of three-year-old Sharon, the apple of her own and Tom's eye . . .

She got up quickly from the dressing stool. It was ridiculous to let such a nebulous cloud overshadow her day; instead she should think how lucky she was, what a wonderful and happy way of life she had compared with so many girls of her age.

Sharon was already downstairs prattling to Tom and Mrs Grey who came in from the village each morning to help with the breakfast and the early morning chores, for often Rose had her hands full with telephone calls before morning surgery which Tom held in the house. Once it had been a Victorian rectory with big high ceilinged rooms and long passages, but in spite of its many inconveniences Rose loved it with the big rambling garden filled with old fashioned flowers, roses, lilies, carnations, filling the summer air with their perfume. There was a grass tennis lawn, rather weedy now, and a wooden summer house with shelves where all down the years apples had been stored so the very woodwork itself seemed to be impregnated with the heady cidery smell. Her vivid imagination conjured up pictures of the people who had walked in the garden in the past, moving serenely past the open French windows. Sometimes Tom would chide her gently for day dreaming.

'You should be called Dream-a-day Jill instead of Rosemary for remembrance,' he'd say, taking her in his arms and kissing her so she felt safe, cherished, far from the dark shadows of the past.

Now he sat in the kitchen which Rose had modernized with pine fittings and a pale blue solid fuel cooker, without losing the character of the place, leaving the glass case of bell indicators with their old fashioned names printed in gold leaf — Drawing room, Master Bedroom, Nursery. She paused for a moment in the doorway looking at the dear familiar scene, a little chill of fear round her heart — unaccountable, frightening.

Tom was tall, dark and ruddy complexioned with curly hair and blue eyes. His parents, and theirs before

4

them, had all been farmingstock, but from the moment he could walk on fat, unsteady legs, Tom had loved all animals and small, defenceless things; he tended birds with broken wings and dogs who had got caught in steel traps which had still been legal when he was young. With scarcely disguised pride his parents had watched him sail through all his exams, through college and medical school, while his younger brother, Frank, took on the family farm. When the local doctor had decided to retire, Tom had, by a stroke of luck, just qualified and came into the practice as a junior partner to Doctor Hale's own son, Pat, whom he had known since they attended village school together. But although there was plenty of work for two on the scattered area near the moor, lately he had felt he wanted to explore further and more specifically the side of the profession he loved — paediatrics, and eventually to teach in the hospital where he had trained. Now a vacancy had occurred, he had applied for it and his appointment hung on a personal interview. Although he would be reluctant to leave Swallowdene he had felt the need for change.

'After all, love, I may be a big fish here,' he had said to Rose, 'but it's a very little pond and there's so much I want to learn, so many people to be helped, and I feel it would be a way of saying thank you for our own healthy small girl. In a way this practice is for someone older than me, someone perhaps coming to the latter years of the profession.'

Rose couldn't explain how she felt — apart from her reluctance to return to London itself for she had grown to love the village, the people, and the farm where Sharon could run wild, where next year, Mary Murray, Tom's mother, had promised to buy her her first pony and to teach her to ride.

'Never too early to learn, love, and it must be in the blood — Murrays have ridden at all the local shows, gymkhanas and point to points ever since time was.'

She was jerked out of her reverie by Sharon who sat at the table in her blue tee shirt and jeans, like something from a breakfast food advert., all golden curls and dewy pink skin, gurgling with laughter now at something her father had said, a delightful, infectious sound.

Tom looked up. 'Hullo, love, we thought you'd gone back to bed.'

Rose turned quickly to take a plate of eggs and bacon from the oven.

'Tease! You knew I'd been down and cooked for you both. I'd only gone to make the beds otherwise they don't get done if that phone starts to ring.'

He nodded, laughing, patting her arm as she put the plate in front of him.

'I know, love. Fortunately Pat's on duty this morning, but I have quite a list of calls before afternoon surgery.'

'It's the fête today; you hadn't forgotten?'

Tom covered his eyes with his hands in mock horror at Rose's words. 'I had.

What will Mum say — a red letter day on the calendar, her cake stand to put up and all the cakes to be collected and delivered to the Hall.'

Rose laughed now. 'Don't worry, you knew perfectly well we were already organized. The only thing is I shan't be here during surgery, but Marjorie's going to come in a bit early to hold the fort.' Marjorie was Tom's receptionist. She had been a nurse until she married the farm herdsman and was glad of the part time job.

'Well, at least you've got a super day for the fête.' Tom looked out of the window, where beyond the neat privet hedge with its white, sweet smelling blossom, he could see his father's fields, filled now with hay bales, the golden stubble stretching away to the purple and blue shimmer of the high moor. He thought for a moment that it would be a wrench to leave all this — but the opportunity was too good to be missed, and perhaps one day when he was too old for the kind of job that he would be tackling at St Benedicts, he could come back and end his days in the more placid daily round of a country GP.

He glanced at his watch. 'Good grief, I must go! Don't keep lunch, Rose. I'll grab a sandwich. My last call will be the other end of the village, and anyway I expect you and Sharon will be eating early to give yourselves time to dress in all your finery for the fête.'

Rose smiled. 'I have made us new dresses, of course, and Mum had asked us to lunch at the farm so I'd be on the spot with the car. I was going to leave you something cold.'

Mrs Grey bustled in from the scullery. She was plump and round and shiny red as a sweet apple, and had lived all her life in Swallowdene. 'Furthest I been was Plymouth on a school outing,' she'd once told Rose. 'Couldn't see nothing to it. Nasty dirty noisy place and you should have seen the price of cakes!' She held up her hands in horror. 'My sister bought what they call a pasty; been ashamed to give it such a name I would if I'd made it, nothing but stringy old trade, not fit for a dog, and tatties as hard as stones. I never been back since and don't want to; me and Fred's got all us wants here.'

Rose was thankful they were content. Mrs Grey was as reliable and honest as a clear summer day and adored Sharon as if she were her own.

'I can make the doctor some lunch, don't you worry, 'tis no trouble.' Tom held up his hands in mock despair. 'I'm overwhelmed by all this female concern for my inner man, but there's no need, I've had an enormous breakfast, and I don't doubt I shall be having an enormous supper. If I miss out a bit in between it'll do me no harm.' With a swift kiss on Rose's cheek and another on Sharon's nose, he was gone, leaving a faint smell of antiseptic and after-shave.

Mrs Grey was singing as she washed the breakfast dishes, Sharon had gone into the garden where she had a small plot of ground Tom had dug for her. She'd planted seeds of brightly coloured annuals, orange marigolds, deep blue cornflowers and many hued nasturtiums, and now with her beloved bear trailing along from one small hand, she crossed in the sunshine to the plants, the air already filled with the promise of coming heat. Rose watched her, and as she did so the telephone shrilled its insistent note.

She went swiftly into the hall to answer it, she was not to know as she lifted the receiver that her life would never be quite the same again . . .

2

It was a man's voice. Rose repeated the number as he said 'Who is that speaking'.

'Mrs Murray. Can I take a message?'

'Rose?' The voice was deep; it awoke some distant memory, and yet she could not place it.

'I'm afraid I didn't catch your name. Did you want to make an appointment?'

'No, it's you I want, Rosie. Surely you haven't forgotten so soon?'

Still she was baffled, she didn't like people who rang and played at being hard to get, trying to make you guess who they were and when you couldn't, taking offence. Little did they realize how many calls she answered a day . . .

'It's Alex — Alex Sutton . . . '

Suddenly the years rolled away — she was a teenager again, and with the memory came an almost suffocating terror.

'Are you still there, Rosie? I'd have known your voice anywhere. I've had the devil of a job tracing you. What on earth made you leave the smoke and bury yourself in such a god-forsaken spot? Talk about being out in the sticks . . . '

'I . . . ' Her throat seemed to have contracted so she couldn't get any words out.

'You don't sound very pleased. I just wanted to see you, have a chat about old times . . . '

'Please . . . I don't — ' It was as if suddenly the solid ground beneath her feet had turned to shifting sand, the world she knew crumbling round her, as if she literally could hear the stones of the edifice she had so carefully built, crashing to the ground. She'd tried — and succeeded she thought — to put away the past, to forget it, to become a good wife to Tom, a loving wife, and a responsible mother to Sharon.

Now — because of the phone call which had erupted into her life, it was all going wrong, everything would be ruined, she knew it.

'I'm married . . . ' At last the words came out.

'I suppose I should have guessed that, it was too much to hope you might have waited for poor old Alex. But that doesn't mean you're shut up in a convent, does it, Rosie? Surely your old man lets you off the lead occasionally. With your looks and flair it'd be selfish to keep you all to himself wouldn't it?'

She had gone deathly cold as if she were about to faint. She sat down on the little stool by the phone. The sounds from the world outside came to her ears in this crisis as something she had to cling to, feeling they should have stopped. She was conscious of Mrs Grey calling a soft 'Cheerio for now!' from the kitchen. Sharon was laughing, shouting, 'Mummy, come and see my new flower!' Cars went by in the lane outside, a pigeon cooed, the swallows

called their high pitched bubbling note
. . . everything seemed sane, the same,
but it wasn't.

'Please leave me alone. Go away. I
can't possibly see you, you must know
that.'

Thank God at least Tom was out . . .

'Oh, so that's the way the wind
blows, is it? Married and under false
pretences in a manner of speaking, kept
our past all locked away nice and neat,
have we? Poor old Alex not good
enough now, is that it?'

'Of course it isn't, it's just that — '

'That hubby hasn't been put in the
picture. I'm surprised at you, Rosie;
always so keen on the truth weren't
you? Well, just suppose I come along
and see him — whatever his name is
— that wouldn't be a very comfortable
few minutes would it?'

'Please . . . ' her voice broke on the
word. It was so inadequate a way to
appeal to Alex, but she couldn't think
of anything else to say. 'Please don't,
Alex.' It seemed strange to say his name

again after all these years. It was so long since she had used it, even thought about him much; the years had brought a merciful haziness — or so she had thought.

'Tom knows all about you anyway so there wouldn't be much point,' she said quickly.

'Tom, is it? Well I think you're lying to me, Rosie, I can tell by your voice, you never were much good at lying were you? I don't think your Tom knows anything about me, or much about the girl he married either. What have you to say to that?'

Why didn't she simply put down the phone? Why did she go on listening? It was as if the instrument were glued to her hand, as though some kind of paralysis prevented her from putting the receiver on its rest . . . patients might be trying to ring . . . Sharon, tired of waiting for her mother, ran into the hall, a purple Canterbury bell in her hand,

'Look! Sharon's flower . . . '

Suddenly she found some strength from somewhere. 'I'm sorry, I can't see you and I can't talk to you any more. Please go away and leave me alone.' Even as she said the words she knew they were meaningless, useless. The instrument slipped from her hands, crashing on to its cradle. Sharon glanced up at her, her face puckered.

'Mummy cross?'

Rose bent down and picked her up, burying her face in the sweet baby smell of her soft neck and fluffy curls, trying to stop the sobs that rose to her throat from somewhere deep inside.

'No darling, Mummy isn't cross, just a little upset.' The child's world was small; little things were important, as they always are to a baby. She grinned at her mother, reassured, and held out the rather battered flower.

'For you.'

Rose took her hand and they went across the hall and out into the garden. For a moment Rose lifted her face to the warmth of the June sun.

'Please God, make him go away,' she whispered.

She had no idea if Alex were in the locality or if he had rung from London, neither had she any idea how he could have found out where she lived, but she supposed it would be easy enough for one of his kind . . .

Now somehow she had to get through the afternoon.

Once or twice she felt her mother-in-law's eyes on her with gentle speculation in their gaze.

'Are you feeling all right, love? You're very quiet.'

Rose forced a smile. 'I'm fine thanks. It's just the heat; I think there's thunder about.' She looked up into the clear blue sky which held no cloud even the size of a baby's fist. Now and then she glanced round with the feeling she was being watched, but nearly all the faces were of people she knew, people who liked her, respected her. She was vice-president of the Women's Institute, helped to run the nursery school for under-fives and, as the doctor's wife the country women respected her for they felt she had a wisdom they didn't possess — if they only knew.

The cake stall was as usual the centre of attraction. Rose had made chocolate sponges — a favourite recipe each year. Her mother-in-law had spent days baking, icing, putting the cakes in the enormous deep freeze they had at the farm, to keep fresh for the day, some of them filled with her own thick yellow clotted cream. Before half of the afternoon had passed they were sold out. In a way Rose wasn't sorry, she had had difficulty in concentrating, in giving the right change, in chatting as if she hadn't a care in the world.

The summer afternoon wore on, people started to drift away, somewhere music wafted from a radio. She remembered reading that when you were young there was something about the long shadows of soft summer evenings that almost guaranteed you'd end up in love . . . the word brought thoughts of Tom . . . and now, memories of Alex . . .

She busied herself with the odd jobs that needed doing, the clearing up, folding up the long trestle tables which had to go back to the village hall, Sharon was absorbed in picking up the paper and cartons which littered the ground. The fête was held in the manor garden; the house was very old, it had been, years ago, the Church House and then the monastery. The garden was formal with little box hedges, roses, great shady trees, a croquet lawn where some of the younger people were playing a game of their own — racing croquet, which would surely have shocked the traditionalists, but which they were thoroughly enjoying. Rose watched them for a moment with envy. Only a few hours ago she had been as carefree, as happy, but now it was as if an enormous shadow had filled the whole of her life, blotting out everything else.

She drove her mother-in-law back to

the farm with all the paraphernalia of dishes, boxes and plates.

'Come in for a moment, love, and have a cup of coffee, or a sherry. You look all in.'

Rose shook her head. Suddenly she felt that if anyone was kind to her she'd burst into tears.

'Thanks, Mum, but Sharon's had a long day,' she paused and smiled at the little girl who was bouncing up and down on the back seat, 'and a sticky one by the look of her hands and dress — and there's evening surgery. It isn't fair to leave Marjorie to cope all on her own with the phone, and Tom's been out all day. You know what that means, a sandwich and a cup of coffee.'

Mary Murray bent and kissed her. If she had been asked she would have said she couldn't have chosen a girl more suitable for Tom than Rose, in fact she'd said as much to her husband Dick, just before the wedding.

'Many people don't agree you lose a son and gain a daughter when they marry, but in our case we're lucky, we seem to have kept Tom and added Rose to the family. However carefully you bring up your kids you can't influence the people they choose to marry!'

'Aye, you're right there,' Dick had agreed. At one time he'd been a little disappointed Tom had chosen medicine instead of the land. Murrays had a long tradition of farming, having come to Devon from Scotland before the First World War, bringing their own Angus and Galloway cattle, which had inter-bred with some success with the Devons, but Frank had taken to farming like the proverbial duck to water, and in the end Dick had become as proud as a pup with two tails of his doctor son. Rose was like the daughter he'd always secretly longed for. Mary had had such a bad time when Frank was born that the doctor had said no more babies. Rose, and then Sharon, had brought him ample compensation for the loss.

Rose drove home slowly. Tom would

be back by now. Surely he'd guess at once that something was wrong. It was pretty certain he had no secrets from her and that he had assumed she was the same. For a moment she drew into the side of the road, she had to have time to get a grip on herself. She dropped her head on her hands, forgetting for the moment the child in the back. Suddenly she felt soft arms round her neck.

'Mummy, don't be sad. I love you and so does Huggy Bear.' She put the well worn teddy bear on Rose's knee. It was all she could do now not to burst into tears. She patted the passenger seat beside her. 'Come and sit here, love. Do up your seat belt, and Huggy can sit in the middle. Mummy's just tired, that's all.' The child leant against her, drowsy now with the long, warm summer day. Rose glanced down at her, at least all was well with her world — for the moment.

3

Tom's car wasn't in the drive when she entered the gates, for which she was thankful. At least it would give her time to change into her old clothes, to try to act normally, to relax a little.

The phone was ringing as she opened the front door. For a moment her heart missed a beat. Suppose it was Alex . . . suppose he rang while Tom was in . . . But Marjorie was answering, smiling at Rose and Sharon as they came in.

Thankfully Rose heard her take a message from a patient for Tom. She went slowly up the stairs and into the bedroom. She took off the blue linen dress which matched her eyes, the high heeled sandals, stretching her toes luxuriously. She put on jeans and a tee shirt. For some reason it seemed easier to behave naturally in her old familiar clothes; she wasn't keen on dressing up anyway. Mary was always saying, 'You're more like a country lass than a townie; it's always difficult to believe your Dad's in business and you were born in London.' And it was true Rose had taken to the way of life as if she'd been born and bred in Swallowdene — it was more than ten years since she and her parents had moved down from London to Plymouth and soon they had moved out of the city to the village where she had met Tom. Four years ago they had married and it seemed now her natural background; that was partly why she didn't want him to take the London appointment — but only partly.

She bathed Sharon and eventually got her into bed, promised that if Tom was in time he would come and tell her a story before she went to sleep. She had heard his car some time ago. He had gone straight into surgery, for, as usual, the waiting room was full. Summer brought almost as many ailments as winter, what with hay fever, and other minor upsets, but Rose suspected that some of the older, lonely folk came simply for a few minutes chat with Tom, knowing that he always made time to listen to them.

She went down to the kitchen to prepare supper. Surgery would probably finish about seven, they usually ate at half past. As she sliced the beans and scraped the new potatoes out of the garden, the sound of Alex's voice filled her mind, and each time the phone rang she felt a shiver of cold fear down her spine. What could she do? She had no one to turn to with this dilemma. Her own mother had died last year — but they had never been particularly close. Now her father had retired in Plymouth. He had a modern flat in one of the more luxurious blocks near the Ho. But neither was he the kind of person in whom she could really confide. She knew she had caused her parents much agony in the past, she'd been young and foolish, and a kind of barrier had grown up between them in the latter years. They were fond of Tom and adored Sharon, and Rose took her to see her grandfather regularly, but there was not the same rapport as she felt with Tom's parents — but that was somewhere she could not turn to, not in this instance.

She made mint sauce, grilled the chops, and just after seven Tom came into the kitchen, rubbing his hands,

'Smells marvellous, and I could eat a horse!'

She stood with her back to him at the stove, unwilling to turn and face him.

'Sorry, no horses on the menu today.' She tried to keep her tone light. He came up behind her and put his arms round her in the old familiar way he had, pulling her against his body and kissing the top of her head.

'And how is my favourite wife? Worn out with all the shindig of the fête, I don't doubt. How about a glass of sherry?'

She nodded, still not looking at him.

'That would be marvellous. Supper's practically ready, but I did promise you'd go and see Sharon, and tell her a story before she goes to sleep. Someone gave her a tiny pair of denims they'd made for Huggy and I think she wants you to see him in them.'

He stood in the doorway with the two glasses of sherry, his eyes on her face now.

'You're looking a bit peaky, love. Are you all right?' It was unusual for Tom to notice — in any case there wasn't anything usually for him to notice; she was healthy and strong. She turned back to the stove.

'I'm fine. It's just the heat.'

'Usually you love it, can't get enough of it.' He put the glasses down. Her heart sank as he came to her once more and turning her round took her face in his hands, looking down, forcing her to look at him.

'There's something wrong. If you're not feeling well please tell me. I can easily get Pat to have a look at you.

There's a lot of gastric trouble doing the rounds, some kind of virus.'

She couldn't tell him — not yet. She had to deal with Alex herself. She had no idea how Tom would react, she tried to think how she would feel if the case were reversed, but she just couldn't imagine Tom in any situation which wasn't absolutely honest and straight-forward. She grinned at him. It wasn't a success.

'Honestly, I'm fine.'

'Well you don't look it. You need a holiday. Tell you what, come up with me when I go to London for the interview, we could make a weekend of it, a kind of second honeymoon. After all we haven't had a holiday since Sharon was born. We could live it up a bit, stay at a really posh hotel, go to a theatre or a club — what do you say?' His enthusiasm for the idea was bubbling over. 'I'll even buy you a new dress!'

She pushed the hair back from her face, desolate at having to hurt him.

'No, honestly, Tom, I'm fine, and what about Sharon?' She gave a weak grin. 'You can't take a little girl of three on a second honeymoon!'

'You know as well as I do Mum would love to have her. I realize she'd be more spoilt than ever when she came back, but the old folk would be over the moon.' He paused a moment. 'I'll go and see Shar. Drink that, it'll do you good, and over supper we'll discuss the idea.'

For a moment as he went out of the room she stood absolutely still. She'd got to deal with Alex by herself, she knew that, there was no way out. She knew, too, that he would ring again. All she prayed was that it would be when Tom was out.

She tossed and turned most of the night, thankful that Tom wasn't too light a sleeper, only where the phone was concerned, over that he seemed to have a sixth sense. She tried to make herself as small possible, rolling into a tight ball on the edge of the bed. Her mouth was dry and she longed for a drink but didn't want to wake Tom. She knew it would only make him pursue once more the idea that something was wrong, for usually she slept deeply and peacefully. She thought the dawn would never come and was thankful when the first birds started to stir below the eaves where the swallows came back to nest each year; the babies were calling for food and the parents already on the wing.

She rolled out of bed and when Tom turned over sleepily and put out his hand to touch her, she made the excuse she thought she had heard Sharon call.

Fortunately, during breakfast Tom was preoccupied with some medical notes he was studying, for once Sharon didn't seem her sunny easygoing self and was inclined to grizzle and act up, something she seldom did, Rose felt guilty, it was probably because she herself was uneasy and edgy, and the child realized it. Kids were so much more sensitive to grown ups' moods and tempers than people seemed to think. Rose was due at the nursery school where she helped out once or twice a week later that morning, and hoped the influence of the other children might put things right.

Tom kissed her briefly and she was thankful he didn't look at her too closely for she knew she had dark shadows under her eyes and even her hair looked drab and colourless. He had scarcely left the house before the phone rang, and although it rang more or less continuously in that house, Rose felt in her bones this was different, this was going to be Alex; it was almost as if he were watching the house and had seen Tom leave. Marjorie wasn't on duty this morning and there was no surgery, Mrs Grey hadn't arrived. She paused for a moment, unwilling to answer, but she knew she had to . . .

Alex's voice said, 'Hullo, sweetie. Glad you had the sense to answer the blower. Could have been awkward otherwise, eh?'

'Look Alex, please, for old times' sake, for my sake, please . . . '

He broke in, 'Now don't give me that, honey. All I want is to see you. It isn't asking much, is it? And that's for old times' sake, as you put it, so where's the problem? And by the way I don't take kindly to being cut off on the phone like you did yesterday; it's not very polite, is it? I'm sure you don't treat your old man's clients like that.'

'Patients — he's a doctor.'

'Patients then; comes to the same thing. Anyway it isn't him I want to talk about, it's us . . . '

This time she broke in, 'It's quite impossible, I can't see you and please don't contact me again. It isn't any use.'

'Now hold your horses, it's for me to say if it's any use or not, and it just so happens that it may be. You see coming back to England I've had to be careful, very careful, the police never give up on a job like this, and although I've changed my appearance and my name, it isn't all that easy. Most of the people

I knew in the old days seem to have melted away — except for you that is, love, that's why I contacted you. I knew, as you just said, for old times' sake, you'd help poor old Alex. I've run out of cash, only temporarily of course, I've got plenty stashed away in South America, but it's the problem of getting into England. These things take time and a lot of arranging, and I need some ready cash quickly.'

'But why have you come back to England? Surely it was safer to stay in Brazil or wherever it was.'

'Maybe, but strange though it may seem to you, I had a hankering after the old country. Must be getting old; it just isn't the same living abroad, specially in those places in SA. It's OK for a bit but it palls.'

Privately Rose thought probably Alex had found he was a very small fish in a big pond the other side of the Atlantic, had spent his money and come back to see if he could round up any of the old gang. She'd heard of it happening in similar cases.

'Are you still there?' His voice had a sharp edge. 'I don't like being cut off, remember?'

'Yes, I'm still here,' she said wearily, 'but it's no use, Alex. I can't possibly see you. There's too much at stake.'

She could have bitten out her tongue directly she had said the words. He was on them like a hawk.

'But I thought you told me yesterday you had nothing to lose, that Tom knew all about everything.' Without waiting for her to reply he went on, 'Well if Mohammed won't come to the mountain, you know what they say . . . I'll be over, so don't leave the house.'

Terrified now in case he rang off and carried out his threat she said quickly, 'No, don't do that please. Just tell me what it is you want. I'll meet you somewhere, but not too far away, I can't leave . . . ' she was about to say 'Sharon', but some sixth sense warned her not to mention the child. 'I can't leave the house and the phone for long.'

'That's more like it, although I'd like to have seen your pad, fallen on your feet, have you? Well, never mind, later on perhaps . . .'

'Tom's a wonderful husband if that's what you mean,' she said with a touch of defiance, 'but doctors are hardly rich in this country so it's no use you getting any ideas on that score . . . and above all I won't have Tom hurt.'

'Well then, just to please you I won't come round, not this time — so here's what you're to do . . . better write it down so you don't forget.'

With trembling fingers Rose wrote down his directions, thankful at least for the fact that at the moment he wouldn't come to the house. She dare not risk that, but for how long could she keep him at bay? The very thought of it froze her blood.

When he rang off she dropped her head on her hands and the tears fell through her fingers on to the floor unchecked.

It was as though her world, her peaceful, happy, well-loved world had suddenly ended.

4

It was a few moments before Rose realized Alex had rung off and the dialling tone seemed to purr with an almost catlike satisfaction at regaining control of the line. She sat quite still, her brain too numb to work. Had she been a fool not to tell Tom about Alex's call in the first place? Surely he would have understood. Or would he? How would she feel if the position had been reversed and he suddenly told her about some extraordinary happening from his past, something quite out of character with both himself, and their present way of life. Could she handle it?

Quickly she dismissed the idea. It just didn't figure, not with Tom — but then perhaps that was how he felt about her, she had been a good wife, she knew that, he'd told her so often enough, and so had Mary — and from a mother-in-law that must be praise, and Sharon was a delightful child, much more than that to her and Tom of course, but she was well-behaved for a little girl of three, popular with other mothers at parties — a good sign. Why, oh why, did Alex have to come back into her life now? Especially at this moment when Tom was hoping to get this job in London. It was the first really sticky patch they'd had in their four year old marriage; no cloud had appeared on the horizon till now. It was something she was pretty certain they would overcome together — or it had been until this new threat arose.

Now she wasn't so sure. If only she could keep the whole thing from Tom, but in her heart she knew it was a vain hope; in her heart she knew Alex too well . . .

She stood up. She had to think, to organize, to plan. First of all she had to find the money. Alex hadn't made any specific demands, but remembering the way of life he had liked, she knew it would be more than she could possibly lay her hands on. She had a few hundred pounds, some of it invested in a building society. Her mother had left her a little money, and she'd saved some when she'd had a job before she married. Tom had insisted she keep it in her own separate account.

'I think a wife should be free to a certain extent, love. Have some money of her own so if she wants to she can indulge a little extravagance now and then without always having to run to her husband for every penny.' Dear Tom, that's just how he would think.

Then there was Sharon. She couldn't possibly take her. For one thing she didn't want Alex even to know she existed — she didn't trust him that far. She knew Mary would love to have her grandchild for the morning, but what excuse could she think up? That her father wanted to see her in Plymouth? But then Mary would know Sharon would go with her. It had to be something convincing, something she could lie about with assurance, and that wasn't going to be easy, although to some extent she knew she had lived a lie with Tom all these years, the telling of direct falsehoods wasn't so easy. Her face always gave her away.

Meanwhile she was wasting precious time. She was terrified if she didn't keep to the strict details of the rendezvous with Alex, he would come to the house.

With clumsy fingers she dressed Sharon in a new cotton dress she had just made for her. It was difficult to keep herself from weeping as she did so. Fortunately the child was fascinated by the animal figures on the material of the dress, gurgling with delight and wriggling like a small eel. For once Rose nearly lost her temper with her. It was only when she'd given her a harder shake than she was accustomed to and the little girl had looked at her with round blue eyes saying, 'Mummy cross again?' that she had hugged her tightly and said, 'No, love, just a bit worried.' She had worked out some kind of story to tell Mary and thought perhaps she'd rehearse it on Sharon.

'Mummy has to go out for a short time, love, and I can't take you. It's to see Mrs Morris — you remember, she has a little girl called Kate. You met her at a party over at South Fernley.'

Sharon nodded. 'I remember. We had sausage rolls and jelly, and after tea we played with her sand heap and I got dirty.'

Rose tried to smile. 'Yes, that's right.' She swallowed, hating herself for lying to the child. 'Kate has measles, and Mrs Morris has to go to Plymouth urgently and she wondered if I'd sit with the little girl until she gets back. It won't be very long, but you see that's why I can't take you — you haven't had measles.'

'Not like Christopher Robin. He had sneezles and weasles and measles,' Sharon crooned to herself.

Rose rang Mary. She felt the lie would be easier to tell over the telephone, it would perhaps soften the glance when she came face to face with those candid blue eyes.

Of course Mary was delighted. 'You've made my day! Whilst I'm sorry the little girl has measles, I was just feeling quite lonesome after the excitement of the fête, and Dick has gone off to market with Frank, so we'll have a lovely time picking raspberries and eating some, too, I expect. Leave her as long as you like. What about Tom and his lunch? Would he like to come here?'

Rose felt as guilty as if she'd stabbed both Mary and Tom in the back with a knife. 'Oh no, he's OK. He won't be home till tonight . . . ' Tonight, she thought, I wonder what will have happened by then. She closed her eyes. 'Please God, make it all right.' She couldn't think of any other words to use, of anything else to ask.

Mary was going on, 'Bring her over just as soon as you like. It's going to be one of those glorious days, so it'll give me a good excuse to play hookey, as we used to say at school, when I should be doing all kinds of good house-wifely chores indoors. Still it's a way of recharging my batteries, and we all need that some times, don't we love?' She chattered on while Rose felt the sweat breaking out all over her body at the thought of what she was about to do.

She decided to drop Sharon before she went to the Building Society Offices for the money. The child might easily make some remark on the fact that they had been there in front of her father, and Tom would wonder why, not that he ever interfered, but she had always told him in the past when she drew out any money for whatever purpose. She could hardly say, 'I took two hundred pounds out of the Building Society today for blackmail money . . . ' A little sob rose in her throat as she thought about it.

Mary was waiting in her gardening clothes with a shady hat, a big bowl and a smaller one in her hands, ready for the fruit. Sharon ran to her and grabbed her round the knees.

'Gran, isn't it lovely? I've brought Huggy; he likes raspberries, but he's promised only to eat a very few.'

Mary laughed and swung the child up in her arms. 'And I hope his owner has promised the same.' She smiled at Rose over the shining, golden head. 'What a shame you have to go and sit indoors on this lovely day! Anyway I hope the little girl won't be too poorly. I'll keep Sharon till you get back so don't worry.' She kissed Rose who was sure she felt exactly like all the other betrayers down the years in history.

She drove into Queensbridge, the market town between Swallowdene and Plymouth where the locals did most of their shopping which couldn't be supplied by the small general store in the village, and where the bank, the building society and other shops lined the narrow mainstreet. Of course all the traders knew Rose and Tom, and the girl in the building society office greeted her with pleasure.

'Hullo Mrs Murray, what a glorious day! Can I help you?'

Rose produced her pass book and held it out, she had just three hundred pounds on deposit. 'I want to take out two hundred pounds please, Jenny.' She was sure the girl must hear her heart beating, it sounded like a sledge hammer in her own ears. But Jenny was too well trained to make any comment, although she did think it odd that little Mrs Murray was withdrawing such a large amount. She knew Rose and Tom seldom went away; they spent any days Tom could take off from work on the farm. He'd smile at people who asked where he was going on holiday, flaunting their tan and murmuring about the Costa del Sol and Marbella, but he and Rose and Sharon got just as brown helping in the hay field, rounding up the cows and generally becoming hired hands, 'We don't really need foreign parts,' Tom would laugh.

Maybe Rose was going to buy some

clothes, or something for the house, Jenny thought as she counted out the notes and stamped the book. Anyhow it was none of her business. She looked up with a smile and was shocked to see how white and ill Rose looked.

'Are you OK, Mrs Murray? You look awfully pale.'

Rose tried a grin which didn't reach her eyes, or her heart.

'I'm fine, thanks. It's a bit thundery, don't you think?'

She wondered how many more times she was going to use that excuse for her looks.

Jenny nodded. 'Yes, I suppose it is. Been a rotten summer, still I've got a week to come in October; maybe we'll have a St Luke's Little Summer.'

Rose gathered up her belongings and went swiftly out to the car. What she was going to say if Tom should happen to pick up her pass book she didn't know; she'd have to hide it somewhere till she could make up the money — if she ever could.

She drove out of the town towards the dual carriageway that led to Plymouth. Alex had told her to meet him at a small pub which stood on the old A38 which had been superseded by the modern road, in a way it was a backwater but it was popular because of its good food and late night discos held in a big barn at the back. Business people from Plymouth drove out for lunch on expense accounts so that it was usually crowded, but far enough away from Swallowdene for it to be unlikely there would be anyone there who recognized Rose — at least she prayed it would be so. The local people didn't often use it and she knew very few people from the city.

The car park was full when she drove the little Mini in, parking it among the gleaming Jags and sports cars, wondering which belonged to Alex. He said he was broke so perhaps he hadn't a car — did that mean he wouldn't be alone, that he had had to get someone to drive him out? She hesitated a moment before pushing open the door that led into the snug where Alex had said he would be waiting. The hesitation was not entirely due to the apprehension in her mind at the rendezvous — it was partly because she felt as though she were stepping back in time, back into the past . . . a past she had hoped to have put behind her forever.

5

Of course she wouldn't have recognized him — that was the whole idea of the change in his appearance, she realized. The disguise was complete. But directly he walked towards her and held out his hands there was no doubt it was Alex. There was something about the way he moved, the confidence in his step, the upright broad shouldered stance, the utter maleness of him that nothing could hide or alter, making her catch her breath for a moment. It seemed odd to see a strange head on the body she remembered so well. Her heart quickened its beat, and deep down inside something long forgotten stirred again into wakefulness at his touch.

'Rosie!' The same smile, the same white even teeth like peeled almonds, the same firm lips, half hidden now by the moustache and curling beard. His eyes looked different somehow, then she realized it must be contact lenses which he wore to alter the colour of the iris, the tinted lens adding a brightness to his glance — Alex with grey eyes which had once been so intensely blue they had reminded her of the summer skies above his head when he had made love to her.

She tried to get a grip on herself, to tell herself here lay danger, terrible danger to herself, to Sharon, to Tom, to her whole way of life, but the old magic, the old charisma held her in thrall.

He led her to a table in the corner where they were shut off from the rest of the bar by a tall settle against the wall. There was a french window opening on to the smooth green lawn where flower beds held bright geraniums and marigolds blooming in the hot sun. She could smell their heady perfume. She sat down and he stood waiting.

'I said, what are you going to drink,

Rosie, the same old thing? Or have your tastes matured a little since the Bacardi and coke days?'

She had forgotten. It had been the 'in' drink in their crowd. She hadn't really liked it, but everyone else drank it and you didn't want to be different, to stick out. She shook her head,

'Just fruit juice, thank you. I've got the car.'

He nodded, grinning. 'Of course, no drinking and driving for the doc's wife. Wouldn't do, would it? The image . . . ' His words were softened by the tone of voice — somehow it didn't sound like Alex. In the old days it would have been mocking, sarcastic, now it just sounded gently teasing.

She sat in a kind of limbo while he was gone. The little bar was full, hazy blue smoke undulated below the low ceiling, voices rose and fell, a girl laughed, someone gave a little scream, whether of fear or delight she didn't know, it all seemed to be in a world she didn't belong to, in the distance, hazy.

She was thankful at least there was no one she knew, and she hoped the Mini was sufficiently hidden that it wouldn't be seen. She had backed it in and left a rug over the bonnet, although why anyone should want to do that on a hot June day she realized was questionable, but it hid the number plate.

He came back with the drinks, hers with a slice of fresh orange and ice — Alex always was a perfectionist. She glanced at his own glass. He grinned.

'I know it looks like plain tonic. Actually it's Vodka, a good drink, because it leaves no traces on the breath. Can't get tequila here; that's my usual poison. Well, Rose, I can't tell you how wonderful it is to see you.'

She lifted her eyes to his at last. They were surprisingly gentle, full of interest. Could it be the contact lenses or had he really changed?

He took out a gold cigarette case and held it open. It contained dark little cigars like cigarettes. Another South American habit, she supposed. She shook her head,

'No thanks, I don't smoke.'

He helped himself to one and lighted it with a lighter that matched the case, the fragrant smoke curling above his head, his eyes half closed as he inhaled the first breath, a habit she remembered.

'No vices, eh?'

'I . . .'

'No small talk either. You've changed, Rosie. You used to be quite a chatterbox. Still, to be fair, I suppose I did catch you a bit on the hop. Tell me about yourself.'

She hesitated, uncertain how much to tell, how much would perhaps play on his sympathy, and how much he might take in to make use of later. She had no illusions concerning Alex, he was a supreme egotist. She had learnt that to her cost many years ago, a lesson hard and well learnt.

'We came to Plymouth soon after —'

'Soon after I went to South America. Is that what you were going to say?'

With a flash of spirit, she said, 'No, I was going to say soon after I was put on probation.'

He shrugged his shoulders, finishing his drink in one swallow. 'OK have it your way — so you and Ma and Pa came to Plymouth. I thought your Dad was an insurance broker. Surely someone like that can't up sticks and away, as it were.'

'The firm had a branch in Plymouth, and one in Bristol. We could have gone to either.'

'I see. Then how did you end up in some god-forsaken little village out on the sticks? I half expected to see you with straw in your hair.'

'It isn't god-forsaken, it's a super place, Mum had chest trouble and Dad wanted to get her out of the city. In those days there was still a lot of smog in winter.'

'And then you met your Tom, the village doc.'

'If you like to put it that way.'

'Well, I'd like to put it your way, but

it seems the cat's got your tongue,' he said gently. Then he bent forward and took both her hands in his. 'Look, Rosie, although I had other reasons, too, I have come partly to say I'm sorry, honest I am. I didn't mean to land you in the mess I did. The whole thing went wrong. Someone grassed; you know how it is.'

She looked him fully in the face now. 'No, I don't know how it is, nor how it was. I only know the whole thing was terrible, ghastly, and that you left me alone to face it. I was only a kid, seventeen, and you knew I'd lived a pretty sheltered life. How you could do it to me I don't know now and I've never known.'

He sighed. 'You must admit Chingford was pretty deadly. Talk about the dreaming suburbs — we were only kids looking for thrills.'

'That might be the way you put it.'

'Your parents never did aprove of me, did they?' He twirled his empty glass. 'Drink up, love. Have something a bit more dashing. I'm going to buy you lunch so you'll have some blotting paper.'

She shook her head. 'No, thanks, and I can't stay for lunch.'

She watched him go to the counter, for a man who was short of cash he seemed extremely expensively dressed — a beautifully cut suit, suede shoes, a silk shirt . . . only the best had always been good enough for Alex. She remembered the first time she had taken him home — in those days he wore leather gear, had long hair and boots with high heels. Her parents had been appalled, her father had told her he was a tearaway of the worst kind, and that he could smell trouble a mile off. Her mother in her gentler, quiet way had tried to deflect her interest by introducing her to whom she considered to be more suitable young men, paying a subscription for her at the local tennis club, the sailing club on a nearby reservoir — but after Alex with his fast motor bike, his way out clothes and his exciting ideas and ambitions, they were like milksops.

'Honestly, darling, you're heading for trouble with that one,' her mother told her when Alex had been fined for speeding and cheeked the police, so he'd had a stern warning. All that had happened was that Rose became all the more determined. When they eventually tried to forbid her to meet him she pointed out she was seventeen, nearly eighteen, and soon would be out of their control anyway, and continued to meet Alex outside the house; there were plenty of meeting places. In the end he was involved in smashing up a café, stealing money from a fruit machine, assaulting a policeman, and sent to Borstal. It was there he became involved with the gang which were eventually to lead to his having to flee the country.

But Rose had lived only for the day he came home from Borstal. He had produced a diamond ring, declaring she was now his girl. It was the proudest moment of her life.

'Look, sugar, there's a rave up tonight. Want you to meet some of the lads.'

'The lads? Not from — from that place?'

He'd grinned and nodded. 'Borstal. Why not say it? There's no disgrace; half the population go through there these days. Kind of College of the Dropouts if you like. Good chaps most of them, my mates anyway, real cobbers. A couple of them from down under. They got plans. We're going to be in the lollie, then you and I can get hitched if that's what you want, have a super pad up west. You'd like that, wouldn't you?'

'Not if it's dishonest,' Rose tried to protest. He'd thrown back his head and roared with laughter.

'Like the geyser said, it all depends what you mean by dishonest. After all who's to say what belongs to who? The Good Book says we come into this world with nothing and leave the same way — not exactly in those words, but I heard something like it at Sunday School. Guess you know more about it than me, so stands to reason anything we get in the meantime's only lent, and why should one person do better than another when we're all just as good as each other?'

Rose wasn't sure about the logic, but anyway she was too much in love, and dazzled by Alex, who was unlike anyone else she had ever met, to question his wisdom. It turned out to be a jewellery and bullion raid the gang had organized. The lorry carrying the goods to the docks was hijacked, one of the Australians drove a bogus police car and diverted it. Rose knew nothing of this, she had been talked into pretending she had a puncture and her car broken down in a narrow part of the side road into which the lorry had been diverted. When the driver got down from the cab to come to her help, Alex had hit him behind with a spanner. The driver had died later in hospital. Rose had had no idea any violence was going to take place, or even that it was a robbery, Alex had told her it was just a trick they were playing on a mate.

Why she should have been so naïve she never knew, but the police had swooped and picked her up and when she looked for Alex, he had gone, along with his two Australian 'cobbers'. They had the money and had disappeared like snow before the sun, eventually to turn up, she heard later, in some South American country from which it had been impossible to extradite them. Rose, because of her youth and previous good behaviour and background, had been put on probation, and that was when her heartbroken parents took her to Devon where she might have a fresh start. It wasn't long before, with the wisdom of passing time she realized the grief she had caused them, and with Tom, and her marriage, she had thought the past was behind her.

Now, as Alex came towards her with

the drinks, she realized only too well that it was nothing of the kind.

But, she told herself, this Alex was different, gentler. The hardness had gone, along with the way out gear. Now he looked like a thousand other ordinary young men, a rep perhaps, even a professional man maybe — like Tom — no, never like Tom.

He grinned, holding up his glass. 'Here's to us and old times. It's good to see you. I really mean that, Rosie.' He covered her hand with his and once again the old thrill she had always felt at his touch ran up her arm like fire.

Suddenly she no longer felt afraid of him; pity, yes, curiosity perhaps, but not fear.

As if he guessed her thoughts, he said softly, his eyes on the handbag which lay on the chair beside her, 'I hate to ask you for the lollie, Rose, but you see I am in a fix until they straighten out the cash bit, and I knew you wouldn't mind me asking, after all we were pretty close once . . .'

She picked up her bag and took out the envelope with the notes. He took it from her. 'Oncers — that's good, thoughtful, like my old Rose.' He started to count them, then suddenly he threw the money down on the table. 'That's a bit poor!' His tone was no longer gentle. 'How the hell do you think I'm going to exist on that? Do you know how much it costs to stay in a hotel for one night? You must be out of your tiny mind.'

Although he was trembling with rage, he had the sense to keep his voice down, which made the whole thing somehow so much more sinister and frightening. 'I thought you said your old man was a doctor? We all know how well the medicine men get paid these days, in their nice cushy group practices — ten thousand plus perks, I bet, with generous housekeeping for the little woman, and you bring me a palty two hundred! It won't do, Rosie. I need at least a thousand, perhaps more. You're trying to make a fool of

me, aren't you? And you'd better
remember Alex doesn't like being
made a fool of.'

He brought his face close to hers. His
eyes were no longer gentle . . .

6

Suddenly Rose was deathly cold and very frightened. She remembered enough of Alex to be able to tell he meant business. She glanced quickly round the bar. Everyone was absorbed in their own affairs. Someone was telling a joke to a little group in the corner. They all threw back their heads and guffawed. What would happen if she went to them and said, 'Please help me . . . '? They'd laugh probably, like they were now, say she looked old enough to fend for herself and couldn't she handle her boy friend?

A young girl and boy sat in another quiet corner, their heads together, talking as only people in love can, oblivious to everyone and everything. She felt Alex's fingers on her wrist, tightening, hurting, his nails biting into her flesh. She looked at him. His whole face seemed to have changed, the eyes now veiled, almost inhuman. She'd seen them like that once before, after the lorry driver had been killed and she had started to scream. He'd slapped her hard across the face so she'd fallen, and he'd left her where she fell, leapt into the getaway car and driven off . . .

'I'll do what I can, I promise, but it isn't easy. Doctors don't get paid as well as some people think, and it's only a country practice with Tom and a partner — and Tom's the junior.'

'Don't give me that spiel — I can tell by your clothes — you've got your own car . . . '

'It's only a Mini, five years old. I have to have it to shop and — '

'And swan around like the lady of the manor, I don't doubt,' he stopped, grinning at the expression on her face. 'That shook you, didn't it? See, I've cased the joint, as they say. I know what goes on so it's no good trying to pull the wool over Alex's eyes. I wasn't born yesterday, you know.' He paused a moment, still holding her wrist, 'and I know you've got a kid — Sharon. Bit of a fancy name, I would have thought, for a country doctor's brat, but you always were a bit on the romantic side, weren't you? You wouldn't like anything to happen to her, would you? Apple of your eye, I expect, and Daddy's girl, too, I guess.'

Rose was horrified at the amount he knew — she had always been amazed at the information Alex was able to glean, apparently without effort.

'You wouldn't dare, you wouldn't touch her. I'll do anything, anything to stop you laying a finger on her.'

'That's more like it. Don't lose your cool — I was always telling you that. No harm's going to come to anyone so long as you just play along and do as you're asked. And at the moment what I'm asking for is a thou. I can't manage with less till my cash comes through.'

'Will you promise me, if I can find that amount of money, that you won't ask for any more, that that'll be the end? You'll leave me alone, go away?'

'Ah, that's asking. I never like to promise anything I can't be absolutely sure of keeping. It wouldn't be straight now, would it? And I can't say for certain how the wheels are going to turn with my finances, these accountants and people are a tricky lot, you know.'

She knew perfectly well he was talking nonsense. He'd never used an accountant in his life, nor was he ever likely to. How he intended getting any money out of South America she had no idea, even if it were true. More likely some of the jewellery or bullion they'd stolen had been stashed away somewhere to await their return. The more she thought about it the more likely the idea became. That would explain why he had come back to England, to collect . . . it was probably in bank strong boxes — she believed that was often done — or perhaps just hidden somewhere. She supposed some of the gang had stayed in England. She

68

believed she remembered that a couple of them had been caught, given prison sentences. Probably by now they were out and they were all going to get together again to pick up the loot. There was nothing she couldn't believe about Alex.

He still gripped her wrist, but his hold had loosened a little now. With his other hand he swept up the notes with a contemptuous gesture and stuffed them carelessly into the pocket of his jacket.

'You don't convince me, I'm afraid. Shame really. If you'd only had the good sense to bring enough lollie in the first place all this wouldn't have been necessary.' His eyes ran over her hands and wrists. 'Got any jewellery you can hock? That's a nice watch.'

She snatched her hand away. It had been Tom's present to her when Sharon had been born, she knew he had had to save for months, going without many little luxuries so he could buy it for her.

'No!' she said sharply. 'Anyway where could I take jewellery to sell it? People would want to know what I needed the money for, and Tom would notice at once if I wasn't wearing it.'

She wasn't sure that was true, but Alex wouldn't know that. He shrugged his shoulders. 'What about the ring? Engagement, I suppose.' He took her hand, gazing at the little diamond ring. 'Not worth much. Didn't think a lot of you, did he, when he bought that? Not like the one I gave you.'

Once again she snatched her hand away as though his touch burned her flesh. 'We didn't have much money.'

'Didn't? I hope that means you've got more now because I'm going to need it.' He got to his feet. 'You're not being very helpful, not very co-operative at all, are you? I'm afraid that means I'm going to have to take you along with me till we can come to some satisfactory arrangement.' He grinned 'And the accommodation I have to offer isn't what I'm sure a young lady like you is used to, but if I can put up with it, so can you.'

She shrank away from him. 'But I can't, you can't do this, I won't go with you. I have to get back, they'll miss me.'

'Not yet they won't, and anyway who cares? They won't have the vaguest idea where to look for you, will they?'

Now Rose was terrified. She felt she would suffocate with horror. He'd taken her arm and pulled her to her feet. The glass doors were open on to the garden and he guided her through them. Without making a scene she had no hope of getting free. She was thankful at least that Sharon was with Mary, and surely as soon as Tom got home and realized she was still out he would phone round and when he couldn't find her, contact the police . . . but how long would that be, and by then where would she be?

When they reached the car park she tried to pull away, but he was too strong, he threw back his head and laughed so that anyone watching would think they were simply fooling around.

'What about my car?' she said desperately.

'It'll be safe here.'

He opened the door of a dark saloon and pushed her into the passenger seat, locking the door after her, and getting into the driving seat. He put the key in the ignition and with his usual expertize, swung the car round and drove swiftly away from the car park, turning off the road and taking a lane that led to the moor.

7

Now that Alex had got her into the car he seemed to undergo a subtle change. The way in which he had talked on the telephone, and then later in the pub, hadn't seemed like the old Alex. She remembered him as gentle in many ways, although perhaps to outsiders he may have seemed brash, his conversation at times even corny — but that had only been after he had mixed with the crowd he had met in the Borstal he had been sent to. But now he was like the sweetheart, the lover he had been when she was seventeen and wildly, ecstatically in love for the first time.

His hand rested gently on her knee.

'I'm sorry, really I am, Rosie. I didn't mean to go off the deep end, but I am up against it and it makes me jumpy.' He grinned. 'Don't remember me like that, do you?'

She shook her head, still speechless from the way she had been 'kidnapped', her mind buzzing like a hive of angry bees with all the thoughts of what would happen at home when she didn't return . . . but his voice was going on and she had to listen.

'South America is a fabulous country — was — if I'd had someone like you with me it'd have been OK. I might have settled down, enjoyed it even, I don't know.' He glanced at the passing countryside. 'Somehow I couldn't settle, and then the money ran out and it's strange really how true it is, the old saying, that home is where the heart is, and my heart was here.' He squeezed her hand. She let it lie in his. 'Of course there were girl friends — I'm not made of stone, remember? The Latin girls are quite something when they're young, run to fat a bit as they get older, but there was still no one like you.' He smiled down at her. 'Don't believe me, do you?'

'I . . . ' her voice was very low, 'yes, as

a matter of fact I do.' She turned her head away as if she couldn't bear to look at him, gazing out across the fields and hedges, bright in the warm afternoon sunshine. Sharon and Mary would be sitting in the garden, swinging gently back and forth on the padded seat with its faded canopy, there would be the smell of warm fruit from the baskets of raspberries they had picked, the two sheepdogs — if they weren't out on the farm with Dick — would be lying in the shade, panting, their tongues lolling out — and Tom — probably going through the notes he had made for the meeting with the Health Authority in Queensbridge during the afternoon. No one would even start to worry about her yet or wonder where she was for hours. She wasn't sure if she was glad or sorry. It depended on what Alex had planned.

He'd turned the car off the main road now, down a narrow lane like a rabbit burrow, the trees meeting overhead making a cool green tunnel, dog roses and honeysuckle spilled over the hedges filling the air with sweet perfume. They were on the very edge of the moor, great granite tors rose in the distance in a shimmering haze of gold and blue heat. Soon they were following what was little more than a track, the car bumping and tossing on the uneven ground. All around were fir and spruce trees.

'Surely this is forestry property,' Rose said.

Alex patted her knee. 'Good thinking. It's a perfect hide out. They've just trimmed the undergrowth and thinned the trees they need for pit props, they won't be back for a year now.' He grinned and put one finger down the side of his nose, closing one eye in an exaggerated wink; an endearing habit she remembered so well. She could smell the sharpness of pine wood, here and there wood shavings lay curled like blond ringlets among the ferns and tall purple flowers of loosestrife. A small stone building stood in a clearing, logs and pit props piled round it. It had a solid slate roof and a squat chimney, a green painted door and a window with a sack tied across it on the inside. A water butt stood by the door with a pipe from the guttering, and nearby, among some rocks, she could hear the tinkle of a stream. If she hadn't felt so frightened, so worked up, it would have appealed to her. It was an ideal place for anyone to hide, a perfect place for a lover of solitude, a perfect place for lovers. She felt a stab of disloyalty at the last thought.

Alex had got out, leaving his door open. He was undoing the padlock on the door, then he came back and opened the passenger door and with a sweeping bow said, 'Come into my parlour, such as it is . . . it's poor, and not mine own, but I have managed some home comforts, and in the fine weather it won't be too bad.'

The moor rose steeply behind the trees and apart from the sound of the stream, there was a still silence hanging over everything with only the song of a bird and the pattering of small animals in the undergrowth. Although it was a hot afternoon, Rose gave an involuntary shiver . . . The tiny cottage smelt musty and damp, but there were, too, smells of paraffin, fried food and woodsmoke — much as it had probably smelled long ago when it was the home of a tin miner.

There was one room downstairs with a ladder which she supposed led into some kind of loft as it disappeared through a hole in the ceiling. The floor was composed of enormous slabs of dark blue slate, probably from a local quarry. There was a chair, a table and a camp bed with blankets and a pillow, a stone hearth where a fire had recently burned, a bucket of water, some saucepans and a bottled gas cooker and a lamp. An old tea chest stood on its side acting as a cupboard for some tins and packets of food.

Alex had watched her as she gazed round, now he put his arm along her shoulders, and she tried to quell the feeling that his touch engendered, it was as if it were an electric wire — a similar feeling she had once experienced on the farm when she had bent to crawl under an electric fence — a warm tingle, but this had something else as well — ecstasy that could not be denied.

'Coffee?'

She glanced at her watch. 'How long are you going to keep me here?'

He grinned at her.

'Perhaps I was thinking of holding you to ransom. How's that for an idea? Think your Tom would fork out, say, a couple of thousand?'

She turned away, her face scarlet. 'Don't be silly. You're talking like a child!'

He came behind her and taking her by the elbows swung her round.

'Look Rosie, I meant all I said in the car. You're in my blood still, you always have been, perhaps you always will, but I do need money badly and you're my only hope for the moment. At least I'm being honest with you, but that isn't the sole reason. I had to see you — to see if . . . ' he broke off as gently she released herself from his grasp. For a moment she was thankful Sharon was safe with Mary; no harm could come to her at least. Surely Tom would contact the police if she wasn't home by midnight . . . he'd ring round all the places where she might be . . . and what would he think when he found she was not where she had told Mary she would be . . . she dared not pursue that thought any further for the moment, anyway that was hours away and it was always possible he might be called out on some emergency and it would be even later that he missed her.

The fragrant smell of coffee filled the little room, Alex put a mug in her hand. 'It's pure ground, not instant. I never did like that stuff, and of course in SA the coffee is quite something — they don't only grow Brazil nuts in Brazil!'

She drank it slowly, savouring the

flavour, then going over to the window, its glass thick with dust and cobwebs. For a moment she watched a bluebottle caught in a web, buzzing, struggling, bobbing up and down in helpless frenzy while the spider watched in its corner, ready to pounce. She lifted a finger to release it . . . before she could, Alex had seized her wrist.

'Don't!' he said sharply. 'I don't want a casual rambler snooping through the window. The dirtier it is the better.'

She turned round. 'I wasn't going to clean it. It was just a poor fly . . . '

He smiled, a tenderness in his eyes. 'You always were the soft one — that was what I first noticed, I suppose. You were so different from the others.' He paused a moment. 'You still are; you haven't changed a bit.'

The mug was clean if thick, and the coffee hot and fragrant. They drank in silence. It was as if the years had rolled away now, as if there'd never been time between.

For a moment she forgot the woman

she was now, she became the teenager without a care in the world, who was madly, helplessly in love, and she put out her hand to touch his sleeve.

'Please, may I go home now? It would make everything much easier.'

He smiled. 'I'll take you back to the pub to pick up your car, don't worry, but not just yet. Surely you can spare me a little time, Rosie. It isn't asking much, a few hours from a lifetime.'

He'd left the door open, and through it she could see the summer afternoon shadows lengthening among the trees. She turned back to him. 'I suppose just a little while wouldn't hurt — now I know you're not serious about the ransom.' She gave a faint smile. 'It wouldn't be much use anyway, we just haven't got that kind of money, but I must get back before Tom thinks he ought to get in touch with the local hospital or the police in case I've had an accident. I'm never out as late as this.' She hesitated a moment, then she said, 'I won't forsake you, Alex . . . '

He took her in his arms now and kissed her full on the lips making her pulse race . . .

8

Her little Mini was still in the pub yard just as she had left it with the rug over it. She did wonder if anyone had seen it and recognized it, but she didn't have time to worry about that now and somehow the morning seemed a world away, it was as if she had lived through a lifetime since then . . .

Alex dropped her a little way along the road from the pub. 'I don't particularly want to be seen there, love.'

She got out and stood uncertainly for a moment in the moonlight. He grinned, his teeth shining white in the silver light.

'Go on, you'll be back. I'm banking on it.' The grin was lopsided, it always had melted her heart, made her pulse race. Now, looking at him, it was as if the years between had never been. She knew he was right.

Now she had reached home and she sat for a moment, her head resting on the steering wheel. Tom's car was there, he was home, and she was terribly late, it was after midnight. She had never felt so tired, mentally and physically drained. She had to have a moment to calm her thoughts which fluttered round and round in her mind like agitated moths. Never in all her married life had she deliberately lied to Tom, or deceived him. Yet, in a way, now she thought about it, she had lived a lie in not telling him of her past, about Alex, and of course as its inevitable result all this had caught up with her now.

She had thought that chapter in her life was closed forever, she had wanted to forget, to make a fresh start, and everything had been done to encourage her to do just that — her parents had wanted it above all for her — and for themselves, but now she wondered if it really had been the wisest course. Tom should have been told, really she owed it to him, with his sweet and generous nature he would have understood, forgiven, even if perhaps he could not forget. He was not the kind of person who harboured a grudge, taunted one with weakness, far from it, all that was alien to his nature. But now it had become impossible to tell him, the opportunity had gone forever, and now she was enmeshed in this tangled web — what were the words she had learned at school from Scott's Marmion — 'O, what a tangled web we weave when first we practise to deceive.' How true the words were of herself!

She tried out the story now that she was going to tell Tom. She had rehearsed it over and over again on the journey home. It was to be a slight elaboration of her original theme — the one she had told Mary about Katie Morris and the measles, and the reason the child had had to be left . . . she was thankful the Morris family were not Tom's patients, they lived the other side of Queensbridge and had a Plymouth doctor.

Suddenly she felt an even deeper sense of shame at her own deception when she thought how she had been cunning enough to work that out even.

Maybe she was Alex's type — not Tom's. He would never have done anything like that whilst Alex would applaud it, and she had even almost forgotten about Sharon — Mary would have kept her, of course, until someone called for her. Tom would have found them both missing when he got home to take surgery . . . she supposed Mary would be the first person he would contact.

It was all so complicated, being devious. Suddenly her life which had been so simple and straightforward had become like a nightmare. To make it worse there seemed to be a warm glow about her as she thought of Alex, the way he looked, his voice, the feel of his hands when he touched her . . . Then remorse — how could she be so disloyal? She loved Tom, he was the father of her child, and yet Alex was like a drug — no, an ecstasy, a fire in her veins. The realization filled her with a kind of horror. Her feelings were stronger than she; what he had done didn't seem to matter, it was as if it had never mattered. She felt again all the old magic he had always held for her. She knew she would help him. She knew she would see him again — soon. She was torn apart. And with this knowledge she got out of the car and walked towards the house and Tom, her lips already forming the lies she was about to tell.

He was in the kitchen in his dressing gown warming some milk, a whisky stood on the table. He seldom drank anything but he had felt the need for 'medicinal purposes' as he told himself with a touch of irony. He'd gone into the sitting room and got the bottle from the little corner cupboard, and as he did so he heard a car in the drive. He took a couple of quick strides across the room into the hall and pulled open the front door. Thank God it was Rose, he had been more anxious than he ever remembered, it was so unlike her to be out at all, let alone until this time. He was filled with an overwhelming relief, quickly followed by a little spurt of anger that the house should be empty and that she hadn't telephoned to put his mind at rest, but she probably had some perfectly reasonable explanation, he told himself . . .

Her face was deathly pale as she came into the kitchen, her eyes two enormous hollows. He took her hands in his, they were icy cold.

'Rose darling, are you all right? I thought you'd had an accident.' He drew her to a chair and pushed her gently down into it. 'Here,' he passed her the whisky he had poured for himself 'drink this while I heat the milk for some cocoa.'

Like an automaton she did as he told her, saying quickly, 'I'm all right, really.' She tried to smile. 'Trouble is I'm not used to driving at night. Usually you're with me and the headlights bother me.'

She passed her hand across her eyes. 'That's all, honestly. Otherwise I'm quite OK.'

He busied himself with the hot drink. 'Mother said you'd had to go out on some emergency, a mission of mercy, she said.' He turned round and grinned. She had dropped her head back against the wall, her eyes closed, but she flicked them open, feeling his glance.

'Yes, Katie Morris, she had measles and her mother had to go to Plymouth, to the hospital, her own mother was ill — it was all rather complicated, but I couldn't take Sharon because of the infection. Was she all right? I do hope she wasn't a nuisance.' How easily it seemed to slide off her tongue, like silk, and she didn't even have the grace to blush . . .

'She was fine,' he smiled. 'You know mother, she'd have her all the time if she could.'

Now she looked at him. He, too, looked tired and drawn.

'Are *you* all right?' she asked quickly, her conscience pricking at not having noticed before, at having left him so long — and the reason.

'Yes, I'm fine really; just had rather a hairy day.' He yawned. 'What say I tell you all about it in bed?'

'I'd like that.' She got up slowly. 'I think I'll have a quick bath.' She lowered her eyes beneath his gaze, she couldn't get into bed beside him with the memory of Alex's touch, the feel of his hands still on her bare flesh.

The warm bath relaxed her a little. She got in beside him. He was sipping his hot drink, the soft light shining on his hair. She felt a surge of intense tenderness for him as if he were a little boy and she years older . . .

'How did the meeting go? Was it as awful as you expected?'

'It never materialized.'

'Oh, did they cancel?'

'No.' He leant back his hands clasped behind his head in an attitude she knew so well which meant he was about to launch into a long story. She closed her eyes. Immediately Alex's image appeared before her. Quickly she opened them again.

She had missed Tom's first few words, but the word Casualty penetrated her conscious mind.

' . . . Pat was there already. The girl at reception at the Health Centre had the message that there'd been one hell of a crash at the Thurstone roundabout, two coaches, one with kids and the other OAPs — and they caught fire, three cars were involved, too, one of the coaches had gone across the central reservation . . . '

'Oh, Tom!' He had her full attention as the awfulness of it overwhelmed her.

'They'd already rung Plymouth for help, but of course some of the victims needed attention. I don't think I've ever driven across town so fast. Thank goodness the law was too busy to watch for speeding doctors! When I got to the hospital already some of the local ambulances had brought in casualties.'

He closed his eyes, she put her hand on his, uncurling the tense fingers and wrapping hers round them in an old familiar gesture, Alex forgotten for the moment.

'Darling, was it awful? A silly question, of course it was.'

'Yes, the burns were the worst part, terrible, many of them on small children, and you know how tiny Casualty is there, it was simply bursting at the seams. The wards were full to capacity with stretchers in everywhere, on the floor between the beds — the place looked like a clearing station on a battlefield.' He paused and then said grimly, 'I must admit I wished I had the Admin. bods from the Health Committee there to see just what the circumstances were. I always knew we'd have a major pile up one day with the new motorway so close, and we needed extensions.'

'And you were proved right,' she said softly, 'but in what a ghastly fashion.'

He nodded, re-living again the scene

with the seemingly never ending stream of stretchers with children and old people in almost equal numbers. Those who were still mobile milled around, searching for relatives or friends, impeding the staff, distressed, desperate, many of them on the verge of hysteria.

'The nurses were marvellous as always, doing all they could with pitifully inadequate equipment — and still the ambulances brought more people. I think both the coaches held at least fifty, but it seemed like hundreds.'

He had carried out a couple of emergency operations, one small boy had to have both his legs amputated — he couldn't bring himself to tell Rose about that.

'There were fractured skulls, crushed limbs, but the burns were the worst. Pat and I worked like a couple of zombies until at last the ambulances arrived from Plymouth and brought us supplies of plasma and saline drips and other things we needed badly.'

'Poor love.' She turned and drew his head down on to her breast.

'I've no idea how long we worked; it seemed like days, not just hours, but when I had a chance to look at my watch it was five o'clock. It felt like the middle of the night.' He kissed the top of her head. As always, her hair smelled sweet like wild flowers.

'Then I had evening surgery. Marjorie's car had packed up and she came out with me. She'd tried to ring you apparently to tell you I'd be late, but Mrs Grey took the message and said she'd leave a note. Of course I found it here when I got back.'

'I'm sorry love, specially as things turned out . . . '

'I was a bit puzzled as you hadn't said at breakfast that you'd be out.' Before she had a chance to reply, he went on, 'just as we were coming away from the hospital David drove up.'

'David?'

'Yes, David Sangster.'

For a moment Rose's heart missed a

beat. David was the local police sergeant at Swallowdene; he and Tom had been at school together.

'Even he'd been shaken by the crash. It was seeing the little kids that upset both of us, although the old folks were pathetic enough, trying so hard not to show their feelings but terrified in case their partner had been killed or seriously hurt.'

'What did David want?' She tried not to sound over-anxious, or even too interested.

'Oh apparently a car had been stolen in Plymouth some time yesterday, one of those dark blue Ford Cortinas — hundreds of them about — but it was seen at the local pub on the old A38, the Wagon and Horses, someone saw it in the car park, but by the time they told David it had gone.'

Rose thought the beating of her heart must be obvious. It must be the car Alex had stolen, and if the person had reported it knew her Mini they might have said so . . . she stiffened in Tom's arms, but he didn't appear to notice and just went on talking about the car.

'David didn't have time to do anything about it, all his men were out at the crash. Anyway stolen cars aren't much of a novelty these days. He gave me the number just in case but I shouldn't think it's likely to be around here, it's probably way up the M5 by now . . . '

God, she thought if he only knew! She must get the piece of paper with the number on out of his pocket, above all she must tell Alex they were searching for the car in the area . . .

Tom yawned and stretched.

'God, I'm bone weary, don't feel much like going off to the big city tomorrow, but it's too good a chance to miss.'

Rose had forgotten about the London appointment — her first thought was that with Tom away it would be easier to see Alex . . . and already she had made the excuse to herself that it was necessary.

'Was Sharon OK?' she said quickly, to cover her own shame. 'She was asleep when I went in just now and I didn't want to disturb her.'

'Oh, yes, fine. She had a wonderful day, I gather Mum had to scrub the fruit stains off her and Huggy is still covered with strawberry juice, but they all seem to have had a good time. She was a bit worried when you didn't turn up after tea, as she expected, but she so loves having Shar that it didn't really matter. She rang me at nine suggesting she keep her there for the night, but I thought you'd only fuss, so I fetched her.' He grinned at her, kissing the end of her nose. 'We are rather a close family, aren't we, love?'

She was glad of the darkness as the hot colour flooded her face, quickly she said, 'How was surgery?'

'Fairly quiet, thank heavens, but I don't know whether it was me — I suppose I was overtired — but they seemed more trying than usual — you know, the kind who come in with a

98

minor complaint which we discuss for some time, and then just as they are going they turn at the door and say something like, 'Oh, doctor, I nearly forgot, you see there's this lump . . . ' and we have to start all over again. Still, as they say in America, that's the way the cookie crumbles.'

Rose rolled on to her back now, watching the moonlight which spilled in through the open window bringing with it the scent of roses from the heat of the day.

It's odd, she thought, when you get up in the morning, facing what you think is going to be a perfectly normal day, suddenly the whole world is knocked topsy-turvy . . . She didn't say the words out aloud — she didn't trust herself — instead with a little sigh she turned on her side. Tom had already started to breathe deeply and she knew he was asleep — she could indulge now in the luxury of thinking about Alex, to remember — and to think of tomorrow.

9

Rose slept badly, her dreams all of Alex so that she woke unrefreshed and not sure where dreams had ended and truth begun — she thought how true it was that no nightmare is as bad when you wake, or dream as good . . .

Tom had set the alarm for five-thirty, as he had to be in London for his interview at ten. Pat had promised to do his surgery for him, but there were case notes to write up and, it seemed, a thousand other things to be arranged.

Rose was edgy and heavy-eyed from lack of sleep, from nerves, and from a guilty conscience. It was difficult to concentrate on what Tom was saying.

'You should have arranged to come with me, love. It would have done you good to have a break. Sharon would have been perfectly all right with Mum — and vice versa.' He grinned at her in the mirror where he was shaving while she tried to wash Sharon's face, the little girl wriggling like a small eel in her grasp.

'Can I go to Gran's again today? There's lots more raspberries to pick, and strawberries — Huggy likes those best.'

'No.' Rose knew her voice was sharp, knew that she must try to control herself, at least while Tom was present.

'No darling,' she said more gently, 'Gran hasn't time to have you every day, and anyway it's tiring for her.'

'I promise I won't be tiring,' she said slowly.

Tom burst out laughing,

'That'll be the day! But don't you want to stay with Mummy? Daddy's going to be away and she'll be lonely.'

Rose felt the hot colour flood her face. She got quickly to her feet.

'Will you have to go to the measly little girl today?' Sharon took her hand and looked up at her, her eyes so like Tom's it was uncanny. She turned away quickly under the pretext of going down to start the breakfast, not that Tom said he felt like eating much —

'Fine thing, a doctor with a nervous tum!' he grinned. 'But so much depends on this.'

Rose didn't meet his glance. Now, with the coming of Alex, somehow the job, leaving Swallowdene, all that part of her life seemed to have faded into insignificance.

Tom sipped his coffee, and toyed with the egg Rose had boiled for him, his mind obviously projected ahead to the coming interview. Sharon watched him with interest.

'Shall I make you some toast soldiers to help with your egg?'

'No, thank you, darling, you eat your own breakfast, I'm just wondering what they'll ask me, whether it'll be questions mostly on what I've actually done here, or what my ideas are on the job they have to offer . . . difficult to guess.'

'Then don't try.' Rose tried to smile, glancing at her watch, wondering what

Alex was doing, whether he was up and about . . . then she wished she hadn't for she felt Tom's eyes on her.

'Got a date, love?' he asked lightly. 'You've looked at your watch more often than I have, and that's saying something. It's almost as if you were anxious for me to be gone.' His voice was teasing, then he said, 'You didn't answer Sharon's question, though. Are you off to baby sit again with what she calls the measly one, or has Mrs Morris managed to make other arrangements?'

'I . . . ' Rose's hand shook as though she had a fever, spilling her coffee. 'Oh blast, and it's a clean table cloth.' She pretended to be preoccupied with mopping up the mess she had made. 'I don't know really, she didn't say last night. She was pretty tired when she got back from the hospital, and her mother's still in intensive care . . . '

'When I get back I'll have a word with Ted Throne at Plymouth General. I know him quite well, maybe I can get some news for her.'

For a moment Rose felt so icy cold she thought she would faint, then the hot blood rushed back to her cheeks. She was a hopeless liar . . . She got up. 'I don't know, I think sometimes it's better just to let people find out these things for themselves — you know — after all, the doctors usually tell them as much as they think is right, perhaps we ought not to interfere.'

Tom looked at her in surprise. 'That's not the way you usually feel! Before, you've kept on and on at me when anyone you know has had someone in hospital, day and night, nagging at me to get the low down or whatever you call it.'

'Yes, I know, but Grace is rather highly-strung, and if you haven't met her — well — perhaps it's best to leave her own doctor to deal with it.'

Tom shrugged. 'Maybe, but if there is anything I can do to help, you know I will.'

He got to his feet, glancing at his watch. 'Heavens, I must go. One thing, it's a lovely morning. No problems there, and there are times when one thanks God for the motorway — others when one does not thank him, such as yesterday, and talking of the motorway . . . ' he felt in his pocket, 'that's darned funny, I thought I put that piece of paper in my pocket with the number of that stolen car on it. I promised to look out for it for David, might spot it on the way to London.'

'I expect by now whoever stole it will have changed the number plates,' Rose said quickly.

Tom gave her a curious look. 'Well, I didn't realize you'd made such a study of criminal behaviour.'

She could have bitten out her tongue, although why it should matter she couldn't really imagine, Tom couldn't have the remotest idea that Alex had stolen it, he didn't even know that Alex existed . . .

'Oh well, never mind, it was only a chance in a million anyway.' He picked up Sharon and swung her on to his shoulder. 'Goodbye my love, and take care of your mummy till I get back — and that bear.' She gurgled with delight as he picked up Huggy and then put them both back on the floor. He drew Rose to him and looked down at her.

'Wish me luck, sweetheart, even if it isn't exactly what you want. After all it would only be for a few years — I know you don't like the idea of London, but perhaps we could find somewhere outside, in the country, Surrey or Kent — and we'll come back here one day, I promise you. It's just that it's too good a chance to miss. I'd never forgive myself if I didn't have a shot at it. You do understand?'

Now she looked up at him and managed a smile. 'Of course, you must do whatever you think best. It's just that life here was so perfect, such a wonderful place to bring up Sharon . . . '

Why had she referred to her life at Swallowdene in the past tense even before plans had really been made to leave?

He kissed her gently on the lips, Sharon ran after him into the drive, Huggy bear trailing along the ground behind her. Rose waited for a moment, unsure, it was as if she stood at a crossroads, uncertain which road to take, as if her life was about to change and the choice was still hers for the moment. Then she ran after Sharon and stood at the door waving as Tom drove away into the bright gold of the summer morning.

Already the heat shimmered above the trees, promising another scorching day. The woods beyond the end of the garden looked cool and inviting, and she thought of the forest and the little cottage where Alex waited . . . and Robert Frost's words came into her mind as she stood there for a moment, her hand on her lips — 'The woods are lovely, dark and deep, but I have promises to keep, and miles to go before I sleep . . .'

She sighed. Now, with Tom gone, she could let herself think of Alex. It was as if by his absence it was made permissible — even as she thought it she knew it was ridiculous.

Sharon tugged at her hand. 'What are we going to do today, Mum?'

'I'm not sure, darling.'

Not at all sure what we're going to do today or all the other days, she thought. Then suddenly on an impulse she lifted the little girl up in her arms like Tom had done and held her close.

'I wonder if you love me, really love me, whatever I may do?'

As if for a second the child had assumed adulthood with its added knowledge, if not wisdom, she put her small plump arms round her mother's neck and kissed her. 'Of course, I'll never love anyone quite like you, not even Huggy . . . or Gran,' she added as an afterthought.

Rose's eyes were filled with tears.

As the morning passed with its usual round of chores and routine, her mind worked on the immediate problem. She scarcely knew what she did, dusting, putting fresh flowers in the bowls, making a pie for the next day, automatically her hands fulfilled their tasks, but her mind was miles away — well, a few miles — at the cottage with Alex. She knew, of course, she would go back again, this time she would take the little bits of jewellery she had for him, one or two pieces her mother had left her. They didn't amount to much; a gold chain with a locket, a bracelet with a little padlock, a couple of rings and a brooch with coloured stones, she didn't know if they were genuine or not. Alex would know. They were pieces she never wore so Tom wouldn't miss them, unless he asked specifically to see them. And that's a stile I'll cross when I reach it, she told herself. Her immediate concern was how to get away without taking Sharon. She couldn't leave her with Mary this time. Even she would ask questions, be entitled to know why

Rose was going out again — and she dared not use the excuse of Katie Morris in case there should be some reason to get in touch with her during the day as Tom was away, and Mary might ring and find her not there and that Katie was extremely healthy and had had measles probably years ago, and her grandmother was not in Plymouth hospital ... for a moment she felt quite dizzy as she thought of the deception she was involved in, the tangled web she was weaving so skilfully, so dangerously.

She made Sharon some fresh orange juice. Marjorie arrived, her little car mended now.

'Hi! I promised Pat I'd come in and help out with surgery.' She flopped down in the old rocker, the rhythmic sound of the rockers on the tiled floor somehow irritating Rose, but suddenly her problem was solved. Even so she couldn't face Marjorie while she said what she had to so she turned to the store cupboard, pretending to be searching for something.

'Marj, would you do me a favour? A terrific favour.'

'Of course, if I can.'

'I have to go out for a little while — to lunch actually, a friend in town. As it's so hot I didn't want to take Sharon — you know how restless and scratchy she gets — and I wondered if I left you some cold meat and salad, would you be an angel and give her her lunch, stay with her till Mrs Grey comes? She's coming in later to make some jam for me ... directly she arrives, then Sharon will be OK with her. I can trust her absolutely.'

For a moment Marjorie gave her a curious look, but it was none of her business. It had just seemed strange yesterday when she had rung the house that Rose should be out. She knew she seldom went anywhere, and if she did she took Sharon with her — even to the hairdresser and the dentist, but she supposed the measle case had been rather different. She got up.

'Of course, I'd be delighted. I've got nothing to do once surgery is over, only a few notes to write up and so on, and I can do that after lunch. Could we take it into the garden, do you think?'

'Of course, make it a picnic.' Rose felt so relieved, almost light-headed at the solution and the fact that Marjorie had agreed so readily that she would have arranged for them to lunch at the Ritz if she'd asked. 'I'll leave everything ready in the fridge, and there's plenty of ice cream and fresh raspberries, just help yourself, and do have a drink if you like to, you well may need it!'

Strange — suddenly Rose's mood seemed to have changed, Marjorie thought, as if some enormous burden had been lifted from her.

'Actually I think fresh orange juice would be as nice as anything, thank you, and now I must go. I can hear voices which means patients are arriving. See you in about an hour.'

Rose glanced at her watch. It was nine o'clock. Surgery would be over by half past ten; she could get away by eleven. It would only take her about half an hour to reach the cottage. She could have six hours with Alex, until Mrs Grey went home . . . she went about the rest of her morning's work with wings on her feet, she felt like a young girl in the flurry of her first affair, a woman who was going to meet her love . . .

10

There had been a few tears as she left Sharon. 'I want to come with you — if not, why can't Huggy and I go to Gran's . . . when will Daddy be back?' Her mouth formed itself into the square shape which always preceded tears, and Rose felt terrible, almost as if she had physically ill-treated her. The silly part was had she been leaving her normally for some perfectly straightforward reason, then she would have felt no guilt, as it was, with the thought of Alex, the anticipation and longing in her whole system, she felt a deep sense of guilt which made her unreasonably impatient with the little girl so that eventually she left in a storm of weeping, clinging to Marjorie and Huggy as if her heart would break. Rose by now was near to tears herself and she drove slowly through the scorching June sunshine.

She had put on a pale blue cotton dress with narrow shoulder straps which showed off her tanned arms and throat, her feet in open sandals, her long legs bare. She wore no make-up except a touch of coral lipstick to complement the tan of her face.

She knew she looked good, but she felt terrible.

In spite of this, as she drove through the summer countryside which smelt of the cut hay lying in the fields, the perfume of honeysuckle and stocks from the cottage gardens as she passed, her spirits lifted as she thought of Alex, only of Alex . . .

He was waiting as if he had known exactly the time she would come. From somewhere he produced a bottle of champagne — typically Alex, she thought with a sudden burst of impatience — he had no money and yet he bought champagne — unless of course he had stolen it.

'Always did have champagne tastes

on a beer income,' he grinned as he saw her, as if he had read her thoughts. He wore an open necked shirt and jeans. He, too, was tanned, relaxed, as if they were meeting in the ordinary course of events on a perfect summer's day — two lovers . . .

The car stood behind the cottage, covered with sacks, he had closed the shutters on the cottage windows so that inside it was like swimming in a fish tank, the sun diffused through the green slats, tiny motes of dust danced in the golden rays where they managed to pierce the shutters. It was cool, peaceful. Alex had produced some cushions from somewhere and made the bed into a day time sofa, a box of fruit stood on the table, and a small bottled gas cooker by the window.

'A poor place, but mine own,' he said with a flourish of one hand as she came in. He drew her into his arms and pulled her down beside him on the sofa. His lips found hers, gentle at first, then more demanding until at last she pushed him away and to her surprise he relaxed and got up. Taking the bottle of champagne he unwound the wire on the cork. 'Midsummer and champagne, a perfect combination, with a beautiful woman.' The cork came out with a little explosion and hit the ceiling, Rose covered her mouth with her hand as she giggled like a schoolgirl. He poured out the golden liquid. 'Sorry the glasses aren't quite right, but I've no doubt it'll still taste good — you always liked champers, didn't you, Rosie?'

She nodded, the bubbles tickling her nose as she drank . . . memory taking her back — she had had champagne on her wedding day — when she was in the hospital having Sharon — and each time it had reminded her of Alex whom she thought she would never see again, for he had been the first person who had bought it for her.

He switched on the little transistor so that music filled the room, and it was as if the years had never been, they were secure in a world of their own. As if it had been arranged, the singer sang the Bacharach tune they had called their own once long ago — 'This guy's in love with you . . .'

Alex stood looking down at her, his eyes glowing.

'You're just as lovely as ever, Rose — and this guy is still in love with you — a rose by any other name — flawless perfection.'

He bent and kissed her eyelids, her cheeks and the corner of her mouth, gently he took the glass from her hand, his lips moved down to the soft hollows at the base of her throat and his hand fondled the silk smooth tanned skin of her shoulder . . . his lips left a burning trail of kisses, her hands reached out to him — and then suddenly, as if someone had switched on a film in front of her eyes, she saw Tom, his face weary after working at the hospital; she thought of his gentleness, his tenderness, his loving compared with this flame of passion, and she snapped back to awareness and a contempt of herself.

So easily could Alex have swept away her resolve, but she had snatched herself back just in time before she let him arouse her once more to the heady peaks of passion she remembered . . .

'Why do you fight me, Rose?' His voice was thick with emotion. She rolled away from him and scrambled to her feet.

'You know why, so don't ask, and don't try to tempt me. I'm in love with Tom, and there's Sharon, my little girl.' Her voice was hardly above a whisper.

He got to his feet and went over to the table. Picking up the bottle of champagne and filling his glass to the brim, he drank it at a draught and banged the glass back on the table so it shattered.

'OK, if you say so. If that's the way you want it.'

With trembling fingers she drew the piece of paper with the car number from her bag, the paper she had taken from Tom's pocket. She held it out to him.

'Look, the local policeman is on to the car. They rang from Plymouth and said it had been stolen and gave him the number, then someone rang to say they had seen it outside the pub, the one where we were yesterday . . . '

He took the paper from her. 'Where did you get this from?'

She turned her head, unable to look him in the eyes. 'I took it from Tom's pocket this morning. He was going to London; I knew he wasn't likely to see the car here, but someone else might, someone walking through the woods . . . '

He grinned now and taking her hand, pulled her towards the door. 'You don't really think I'm as thick as that, do you, love? Come with me.'

He pulled back the bolt and opened the door. Hot sunshine streamed into the little room making Rose screw up her eyes at its intense golden heat. Still holding her hand he drew her after him round to the back where the car stood. He lifted one of the sacks and pointed to the number plate.

'There, compare that with your piece of paper the fuzz gave you.'

Slowly she read out the number on the paper — it was completely different. He kicked at a stone with his toe.

'Trust old Alex. I changed them last night. The colour of the car doesn't matter. There's thousands of this make exactly the same.'

She had brought a basket of food. She'd had to fill it while Sharon was safely in the garden, hiding it in the car before Marjorie came, hating every moment of the devious way she was behaving, and yet hardly able to wait for the time when she would be with him again.

There was cold chicken, home made rolls, fresh cos lettuce and spring onions from the garden, tomatoes and cucumber from the little greenhouse that was Tom's pride and joy . . . an apple pie and rich golden cream from the farm.

He ate as though he were starving.

'I'd forgotten how good English food can be, specially country food.' He smiled at her, leaning his back against the moss covered bark of a tree, an oak which had escaped the axe when the wood had been cleared and replanted with conifers more than twenty-five years ago.

'Suppose someone comes,' she said, looking round almost as if she expected a party of ramblers to appear at any moment.

'No fear of that; it's private, belongs to the forestry people, and they've cleared the undergrowth lately, as you can see. That means they won't be back for months, perhaps years even. Anyway I checked to see where the local folk were. I rang their office just in case, and they're miles away.'

He grinned at her like a small boy and her heart turned over once more. But as if to prevent herself weakening, she said, 'I wish you could see my — our — little girl, Sharon. She's really quite something. I know all mothers think their children are different, but it isn't just me, everyone in the village loves her.'

He shrugged. 'I suppose kids are OK in their place. Never went for them much myself. Too much of a tie and look what they cost to keep and educate.'

'You don't think about that when you have them. There's no feeling in the world like being a parent, having something of your very own, someone you've created from love . . . '

He got up abruptly and held out his hand. 'Come on, I'm going in to make some coffee.'

She cleared up the remains of the picnic and packed it into the car. Soon she would have to think of going back . . . home . . . She took the box of jewellery she had brought from the glove compartment. Was she mad to give it to him when he could buy champagne? It just wasn't consistent, rational, the same as he had always been. She pushed the box back into the compartment. She wouldn't give the jewels to him. Why should she? They might not be worth much but to her they had a sentimental value.

She hadn't heard him come up behind her. He put his hand on her arm.

'What have you got there — Rosie? Goodies for Alex?'

He snatched the box from her and opened it, pouring the contents on to the ground. 'Mm, not much of value there, still they might keep me going for a day or two, I shall have to go back into Plymouth, I suppose, to hock them. Too dicey round here. Shan't get a lot for them, shall I? Is that the best you can do?'

She felt the stinging tears behind her lids.

'Oh, please, Alex, don't be like that. You know I haven't got anything else.'

Like cloud shadows moving across the grass, his mood had changed again.

'I must go,' she said, reluctant to break the spell, to leave, not knowing how on earth she was going to manage to come back again, to make excuses to Tom.

He stood looking at her as if he were reading her mind. 'Do you remember that summer when you were sixteen? We used to go to the park. We were like a couple of kids, playing hide and seek. I remember one particular evening we had stayed out so late they'd locked the gates and we had to climb over. The first stars were coming out.' He paused a moment, then he said, 'There's something about an English summer evening you don't get anywhere else — the long shadows that guarantee you'll end up in love . . . remember?'

She remembered. It was difficult to believe now that someone like Alex should do so though — tenderly, and use such words to describe his feelings. She hadn't realized it had meant so much to him — the blue and gold of a summer day meeting the dusk of night, like it said in the old song.

Once more a surge of love flooded

through her. She longed to go into his arms again, to be held there forever, to forget everything else, even Tom and Sharon, her life in Swallowdene.

She turned quickly and got into the car.

He stood holding the door, looking down at her, but now his eyes were cold like pebbles beneath a stream. He drummed with his fingers on the roof.

'You'd better find some more lollie, Rosie,' he said. 'It'll be a little while till I get myself sorted out — and you wouldn't like me to have to go to your Tom and ask for bread now, would you?'

She let in the clutch and the car leapt forward. She couldn't trust herself to speak. She knew well enough that if it came to the crunch, he would do exactly that . . .

11

Tom returned from London over the moon with excitement. He'd been gone two days and the house seemed empty without him, almost as if it waited silently for his return. Rose loved every nook and cranny of it and the thought of leaving it was like a knife in her heart, but even the idea of going to London and all that entailed had paled a little into insignificance with Alex's arrival and their meeting.

She felt so guilty about him that she tried to meet Tom's exuberance on mutual ground, and when he suggested a night out she couldn't refuse . . . all the time, too, she lived on a knife edge in case Alex should ring or get in touch somehow or other while Tom was in the house, although when she thought about it later she realized how foolish she had been; the last thing he would want to do would be to lay himself open to any chance of capture. So long as he lay low it was unlikely he would be found. On the face of it, apart from the stolen car, the police had no reason to be looking for him, unless his re-entry into the country from South America had been noted, which wasn't likely as he was travelling on a false passport and certainly his appearance was altered from the man who had left in so great a hurry many years before. However that didn't prevent Rose from having many sleepless nights as she lay beside Tom, who slept like a baby, his breathing quiet and even while she watched the moon on its journey across the sky, wondering what the future held.

She met him at the door when she heard his car in the drive. She had put Sharon to bed and waited to grill the steaks until he arrived — 'Hope to be back about ten, love, but you know how uncertain it is travelling this time of year with the traffic,' he had said over the phone, and she had even caught a little of the excitement at the sound of his voice. After all, whatever she might feel personally, it was a terrific feather in Tom's cap — a little known country GP to have the chance of a plum job in a teaching hospital in competition with the rest of the medical profession.

'Not that I'm really surprised,' she had said to him when he told her on the phone that he thought at least he was on the short list. 'I know you're the best.'

'Bless you sweetheart, for the vote of confidence,' he had said, laughing. 'To me your opinion matters more than theirs . . . '

Now she ran into his arms, suddenly glad of the haven of their warmth as they encircled her, certain for the moment of where her love and happiness lay, surprised she could have thought otherwise . . .

'Darling, it's lovely to be home, awful journey . . . ' He put down his case at the foot of the stairs and turned back to her. 'I'd give a year's pay for a drink, long and cool . . . '

'I know just the thing — a Campari soda,' she said, going to the cupboard for the drinks, 'then a steak and salad, raspberries and cream. How does that grab you?'

He laughed and drew her back into his arms, smothering her face with kisses, all the past tension and doubts forgotten. Then he followed her into the kitchen and sat sipping his drink while she cooked the meal, describing the details of the interview. For a moment she tried to imagine Alex in such circumstances, and couldn't . . . Tom ate his food with obvious relish.

'Nothing like home cooking. You can keep all that hotel and restaurant food,' he grinned at her, patting his stomach as he sat back replete. He lit a small cigar which occasionally he allowed himself, the fragrant blue smoke floating in slow rings to the ceiling.

'Well, that's about it. I should hear

within a week if they think I'm right for the job.'

She got up quickly, unable now to meet his eyes, once more unsure of herself, and her true feelings.

He rose as well and went over to her, taking her by the elbows and swinging her round, off the ground.

'Rose, this is something we're going to have to come to terms with — perhaps even with each other and our relationship as well . . . '

Still she couldn't meet his gaze, something that had never occurred before. He released her and took her face between his hands so she had to look at him.

'Is there something wrong? Something more than just your worry over leaving Swallowdene?'

She felt the warm colour rising to her cheeks and said quickly, 'No, of course not, but I love it here. I thought you did, too. After all it's more your home than it is mine really, but I always feel as if I was meant to be here, as if I belonged . . . '

'You do, of course you do, but try to see it my way, love.'

She drew away from him and went to the sink, starting to wash the dishes, glad to be away from that candid gaze.

'Here it is a pleasant enough little backwater, people suffer from the usual diseases, they are born, they die — it's the world in a microcosm — but only that. Out there, in the third world for instance, children are dying as soon as they are born, almost before even, there is so much disease, so much misery, so much to be done and in my own small way, with the research, the teaching, I feel I can help. Let's face it, we are living in a kind of lotus land here, I'm doing a job a man twice my age could perform perfectly, something I could come back to when I'm nearly due for retirement.'

She swung round.

'I thought at the worst it would only be for a few years,' she burst out.

He shrugged his shoulders.

'I suppose it depends on what I make of it. A teaching and research hospital has many opportunities, many facets. Don't you see, love — it's the kind of life any young doctor would give his back teeth for.'

'Yes,' she said slowly, 'I can see that.' She paused a moment and then said, 'I suppose it's a matter of getting your priorities right, and where they lie . . . you see I feel that one's family — close family — comes before anything and that this is the place for Sharon to be brought up — and for us to have more children — I want two more and I thought you did, and what kind of life will it be for them in London? I know the old idea of smoke and polluted air isn't perhaps as bad as it was, but you still can't compare it with the fresh air, the open sky, the fields and woods here where they can roam about without having continuously to be watched as they would in a city — after all, I do know, I lived there myself.'

He got up and stretched. 'I'm tired, Rose, and you must be, too. Let's not discuss it any more tonight, eh? There'll be time tomorrow and the next day, I don't have to decide until I hear from them anyway.' He paused a moment, some of the joy drained from his face, making her feel guilty. 'After all, I'm probably being very optimistic, they may not even really consider me beyond the short list.'

She went over to him, drying her hands on her apron, and putting her arms round his neck said, 'Of course they'll choose you; they'd be morons if they didn't.'

He nuzzled her neck and whispered, 'Come on, let's go to bed. I can think of better ways of spending our time than discussing something which at the moment is nebulous.'

Arms entwined, they went upstairs, glancing in at a sleeping Sharon, Huggy as always close beside her, before going into their own room and softly closing the door.

* * *

Every time the phone rang during the next few days Rose half expected it to be Alex. She hadn't told him when she would be back to see him at the cottage, or even if she would, and now she felt she must stay by Tom's side and give him all the love and support she could while he waited on tenterhooks to hear from the hospital governors.

Usually if the phone rang during surgery hours, Marjorie answered for there was no separate line for the house — and now if she'd done so Rose waited with bated breath, stopping whatever she was doing to listen in case Marjorie should call her, probably wondering who the man ringing her was. But three days passed and there was no message, no sign from him. She was lulled into a sense of false security, sometimes thinking perhaps she imagined or dreamed the whole thing.

Then one day as she was going into the garden to pick some roses for the bowls in the sitting room, she saw David coming up the drive in his Panda car. Her heart missed a beat . . . had he found out about her and Alex? Had Alex been discovered? Had he told David about the money and jewellery she had taken him? She felt guilty every time she went to the little box where she had kept the trinkets, now empty and reproachful.

He drew up beside her and leaned from the window, grinning.

'Hi, there! Isn't it a fabulous day? True June and only England can put on such a brilliant show.'

She felt some of the tension dispersing. Surely he wouldn't be so friendly if he knew she was guilty of being an accomplice, or whatever they were called. She wondered if he had details of her past on file. Did they send these out to the local police stations? She didn't know. One heard such stories about central computers, and the information fed into them and distributed. Anyway if so he was a good actor for he gave no sign of anything unusual, in fact he reminded her of a big friendly puppy; he was tall and had run to fat since giving up rugger and cricket.

'Getting up along now, too old and creaky for all those things,' he'd said laughingly one day when he'd seen her on her way to play tennis.

Now he said, 'Tom in? I wanted a word in passing.'

She nodded. 'Yes, he's just finished surgery. Don't tell me you've come to arrest him?'

He grinned. 'Of course. We found cannabis at the bottom of the garden!' He threw back his head and laughed, climbing out of the car and standing with his hands on his hips. At that moment Tom came out to his car, case in hand, swinging his stethoscope in the other.

'Hullo! What have we done now?' he said, and David slapped him on the back, nearly knocking him flying. 'Steady on, you don't know your own strength!' Tom protested.

'Why is it that everyone has such a guilt complex? They've only got to see a copper and they immediately think he's come about some transgression. Must be a moral there somewhere!'

'The moral is that we're all human, we are all potential criminals and we can never be sure we haven't parked in the wrong place, not paid our rates, or forgotten the TV licence!' Tom laughed at him.

'The last two apply to coppers just as much as non coppers. Anyway, this time you needn't feel guilty — that is unless you've seen the car I asked you about and not reported it.'

Suddenly Rose was deathly cold. She actually shivered. It was something she had forgotten for the moment — now the memory and danger of it came flooding back.

'Oh yes,' Tom said, stopping in his tracks and feeling in his top pocket. 'Of course, you wrote the number down for me. I had it in here . . . ' Then he felt in his other pockets. 'That's odd. Did I wear this suit to London, Rose? I can't remember.'

She tried to act normally, as she said, 'Of course, darling. You only have two.'

'Then I must have dropped it.'

'Perhaps you pulled it out with something else,' she said quickly.

'Unlikely. I don't keep anything else in that pocket, and it was a whole sheet from David's notebook, I'd have noticed . . . damned funny . . . '

'Well, by this time it's sure to be out of the neighbourhood anyway, but I just thought you might have heard something from someone else perhaps, even if you hadn't seen it yourself. It's surprising how often people do notice car numbers, specially kids . . . '

'Didn't you say it had been seen outside a local pub?'

'Yes, the Wagon and Horses. Seems a couple had gone in for a quickie and left their small boy in the car. He's a number plate collector. You know, they have competitions to see who can reach a certain number in sequence first, and this one happened to be a Plymouth number he was looking for.'

Rose felt dizzy at his words — in that case the child would have noticed her number — that Mini was second-hand and had come from London . . . but David was going on.

'Anyway I put out a call to all patrols, of course, but it was just about the time of the pile up and everything had got chaotic. Funny thing is I've got a kind of feeling about this. I'm certain it's still in the area or someone local has seen it. I know it's a common enough car and colour, but as I say, there are people who notice these things . . . '

'Well, I'm sorry, old lad, I can't be much help. Still, I hope you find it. Must be rotten to have your car nicked.'

David nodded. 'Trouble is it's such a common occurrence now. It's like the pile up — the paper hardly gave it any space — they never do unless about half a dozen people are killed. We seem to have lost all sense of the values in life somewhere along the way.'

Tom got into his car and shut the door, then he wound down the window.

'You can say that again,' he said. 'Well, have to be off. See you.' With a wave of his hand he was gone.

Rose stood irresolute. She'd never felt awkward with David before, now she was sure he must see right inside her guilty head, which she knew was ridiculous, but she was convinced that at least her face must give her away; she had never been good at dissembling. She knew she should ask him in for a cup of coffee, but she couldn't bring herself to — she wanted him gone as quickly as possible, terrified of what he might say next.

He stood looking at her for a moment as if he, too, thought she would offer him some refreshment, then the small radio he carried started to crackle and a voice came over the air. He got into the car and lifted the phone, and after a few words, turned to Rose.

'Must go, duty calls. See you.'

With an intense feeling of relief she saw him drive away, and then wondered again if it was news of Alex or the car which had reached him.

She went quickly indoors, telling herself there was no reason on earth it should be either . . .

12

Rose felt restless, all the time playing a kind of double role, torn between her love for Tom — and all the old feelings that seeing Alex had aroused again. They had lain dormant for many years under the layers of happy and contented respectability, of normality — but now in the back of her mind was a little niggling feeling — was her life dull and ordinary? Tucked away in a village where the Summer Fête, Harvest Festival, the odd barn dance and local cricket match were the highlights of the year — should she want something more?

Never before had such thoughts invaded her mind, but Alex had aroused old memories, old wounds had been re-opened. She knew that whatever did happen, she could not hand him over to the police, he was too much part of the fabric of her past . . . she couldn't forsake him — neither could she return to him.

The greatest problem was that as long as he remained in the cottage he was a source of danger, a threat, to her present way of life, and yet she had to see him to try and keep him quiet until such time as he moved on. She knew, too, that she would have to take him money each time she went, at least enough to keep him quiet until whatever he was expecting materialized — at least these were the reasons her heart gave to her head . . .

It was then the idea came to her — she would enrol in some evening classes in Queensbridge — that would give her an excuse a couple of times a week to go and see Alex, even if only for half an hour. She could slip away early to the class and still attend it in case Tom should query it . . . the more involved she got, the more devious she became and the more she worried and knew she was becoming edgy and jumpy. She snapped at Sharon, something she had never done before and could have bitten her tongue out when she saw the way the child recoiled from her, her eyes wide with surprise and fear.

She collected some brochures from the library and when Tom came home was busy reading them. He flopped on the sofa beside her and picked one up at random.

'Yoga — day and evening classes . . . what's this then?'

'I thought I'd go to a class of some kind — either pottery or painting, to get me out of the house for a little. Sometimes I do feel a bit cabbage-like.'

He put his arm round her.

'Haven't you enough to do with Sharon and me to look after? And the house and garden . . . I don't want you wearing yourself out,' he paused a moment, 'and it may be we shan't be here by Christmas, love. You have to face that possibility, you know.'

He still hadn't heard from the

hospital, but Rose dreaded the post coming in case the confirmation arrived. It was a kind of love/hate relationship, just another complication added to her life at the moment. She got up impatiently.

'They're only short courses; the main ones start in the autumn, these are just kind of fillers. I'd like to do something artistic. I used to be quite good at art at school.'

'Of course, if you feel like that about it.' She knew her voice had been petulant.

'How about Sharon? Shall you leave her with mother?'

'I suppose I could, but Marjorie perhaps would baby sit as long as it's not surgery night.'

'I don't think it's really fair to ask her; she puts in a pretty long day as it is.'

'Well, she can always say no!' Immediately she regretted the sharpness, but it was too late.

'Rose, if all this is because of the new

job, we're going to have to come to terms with it — with each other . . . '

She was about to say, 'It isn't really that . . . ' but bit back the words just in time. 'I can't see there's anything specially awful or odd about wanting to have a little life of my own!'

'Of course not.' He was immediately contrite. 'If that's what you want, why not? I'm being selfish, worrying in case I don't get your full attention, like Sharon.' He grinned and kissed her cheek. 'You get fixed up. Anyway . . . ' he shrugged his shoulders, 'maybe the job will fall through.' For a moment his shoulders drooped and he looked so dejected she felt a surge of love and compassion.

'Darling, I'm sure it won't. Anyway I must get the supper.' She went through into the kitchen feeling that nothing had been resolved, but at least she had broken the ice as far as the classes were concerned. Tomorrow she would go and make the necessary arrangements. Perhaps as soon as the day after she could see Alex again . . . the thought made her pulse beat a little faster.

There was only one place left in the pottery class. She had thought it would be easy to get in, but the young man who interviewed her and gave her the forms to fill in said, 'Usually by this time all the places are gone, people seem to find throwing pots very relaxing, a kind of therapy. But someone has fallen out so you're lucky. Actually we started the short sandwich course a couple of weeks ago, but I expect you'll pick it up.' He glanced at her pale linen dress and sandals. 'You'll need an overall; it can be pretty messy.'

The class was next evening and she started to count the hours until she would see Alex again.

When she got home the phone was ringing . . . it was Mary.

'Hullo, we haven't seen you and Sharon for a couple of days. Any news of Tom's job?'

Rose knew her mother-in-law felt much the same as as she did. She didn't want Tom to leave the village, and yet she was proud that he had the chance of such a good job.

'No, I'm sorry, I have been rather busy.' She was about to tell Mary about the class when her mother-in-law went on.

'Well never mind, but I hope you can come over tomorrow evening. We're discussing the arrangements for the old folk's outing next month, and I would like you to take a few notes and help with some of the arrangements with the bus people and so on. We thought we'd take a picnic for them — nothing elaborate, but in small individual packs so they can each have their own; it's much easier that way, and they like it better than a café. The food's so awful these days, and such a price . . . ' She went rambling on, but Rose had stopped listening . . . tomorrow evening . . . tomorrow she was seeing Alex.

She waited till Mary had finished, trying to concentrate, but suddenly realizing she had stopped talking, as she said, 'Rose . . . are you there, dear?'

'Oh, yes, sorry. I thought I heard Sharon calling . . . it's a bit awkward tomorrow. You see I've arranged to go to these classes . . . '

'Classes? Whatever for, dear? Surely you've got enough to do, and if you haven't I can find you lots of jobs. I'm always wanting help with meals on wheels, and organizing the bingo and whist drives in the evenings. I haven't pressed you because I thought you had so much to do and couldn't leave Sharon. Is this some new idea? And what shall you do for a baby sitter? What does Tom think about it?'

Rose felt a growing irritation. It seemed she was not expected to have any life of her own. She knew the classes were only an excuse for her illicit meetings with Alex, but just suppose it had been a genuine idea — that she had wanted to go out one evening a week, just for her own pleasure . . .

'They're pottery classes, and I was

lucky to get in. It's only because there's been a cancellation.'

'Oh.' Mary sounded taken aback by the brusque tone of her voice. 'I see. Well, I suppose if that's the case . . . '

'I'm sorry, any other evening.' She was determined not to weaken.

'I'm afraid no other evening will do. It's a question of when the vicar can manage.'

'I am sorry.' She knew she didn't really sound it, but she couldn't give up now.

'Oh, well, I shall have to find someone else, I suppose. I always thought I could depend on you, Rose.'

She rang off and Rose felt like a pricked balloon, but it was too late to go back now.

It seemed suddenly as if fate itself were conspiring against her for the next morning, after she had arranged for Marjorie to baby sit in the evening, a member of the parish council rang to ask her if she would be responsible for a stall at the jumble sale the next week; it seemed someone had been taken ill.

'It's the second-hand bookstall. Usually it goes like a bomb. I'm sure you'd enjoy it, dear.'

That, too, was a Wednesday, the night she had arranged for her class. It just didn't seem possible things could work out so badly.

'I'm so sorry, Miss Moss . . . ' She seemed to be spending her life now making apologies.

'Oh my dear, don't say no. I was depending on you. You've never let me down before. We all think of you as so dependable, such a nice girl, so much part of the community life here.'

'Well, I'm afraid you'll all have to change your minds — you see Tom's thinking of taking a job in London so we may not be here much longer anyway.'

She knew she had no business to talk about the job, and certainly not to Miss Moss who was a noted gossip, but she felt at the end of her tether. Why did they all have to pick on the one evening in the week that mattered? It was almost as if it were deliberate.

Marjorie, too, had been dubious about baby sitting.

'I was going to catch up on some painting at home — decorating, I mean,' she added rather meaningfully when Rose had explained it was a pottery class she was attending. She could tell from her tone she thought it was a waste of time, a whim on her part, but in the end she had rather reluctantly agreed.

Rose wondered what she would do next week — she felt Marjorie couldn't be cajoled into another stint, and Mary was already a little annoyed with her. It was if she had got out of step with everyone, fallen from grace. Oh, well, she thought, perhaps it will be just as well if we do go to London. A lot they all care when I ask for a little consideration for once . . .

But in spite of such thoughts, she knew in her heart it was because what she was doing was wrong . . . By the afternoon she didn't care. All she cared was that she was going to see Alex again.

Tom came home at lunch time and she could tell by his face he was angry, a rare occurrence. He came straight to the point.

'I've just seen mother. She said you refused to go and help her this evening. Surely that class of yours could wait? Is it all that important?'

Rose's nerves were already raw with the various complications which had arisen and now she turned on him.

'I can't see why everyone else can have time to do their own thing except me. It's the first time since we've been married I've ever struck out for myself, and all of you — the whole village — seem to be set on stopping me. Well, you can all do what you like, I'm going and that's that.'

She ran from the room and upstairs, banging her bedroom door and flinging herself on the bed, bursting into tears as she did so. She didn't know how long she lay there until she felt drained at last of all anger, all emotion . . . She sat up and dried her eyes. She looked a sight in the mirror. What would Alex think? Would the puffiness have gone by this evening? She had half expected Tom would come to seek her out, but evidently he must have given Sharon her lunch for the child was out in the garden with Huggy and her pram, pushing it round the paths, singing quite happily to herself.

Even she doesn't need me, Rose thought bitterly. She washed her face and put on some lipstick, then slowly she went down the stairs. Tom stood in the hall, having just put down the phone. She expected some form of comment on her absence, but to her surprise he was beaming.

'That was the hospital, the job's mine!' he exclaimed. 'They're sending through the confirmation by post, but they thought they wouldn't keep me in suspense any longer.'

He picked Rose up and waltzed round the hall with her. 'Isn't it marvellous? Tonight we'll go out and celebrate like I promised, champagne, the lot!'

She didn't reply.

'Darling, please be a bit pleased for me,' he said quickly. 'Honestly it won't be as bad as you think, leaving here . . .'

He put her down and she turned away from him.

'I can't go out this evening. You know I can't. It's my pottery class, the first one. I can't miss out on that.'

For a moment he didn't answer, then, as if he were keeping his temper under control with enormous difficulty, he said in an icy tone, 'It's my belief there's more behind all this business than you tell me. If that's all you can feel then perhaps it would be better if I went to London on my own!' Without another word he turned and went out to the car, slamming the door and driving away before she had time to move. Now from somewhere deep inside her rose a suffocating feeling — for a moment she wasn't sure what it was, then with a shiver she recognized it as panic . . .

13

As the day wore on Rose forgot — or almost forgot — about her row with Tom, which in itself was strange for they had never really had a serious quarrel before — but she could only think of her evening with Alex which lay ahead.

First though, she had to get some money from somewhere. There couldn't be much left in the Building Society. She did share a current account in the bank with Tom, the one she used for housekeeping — but the cheque needed both their signatures.

Even before she acknowledged it in the forefront of her mind, she knew what she was going to do.

She went into the surgery and looked for some of the papers and forms which bore his signature. With a pen she traced the letters, concentrating on the work so much that she didn't hear Sharon come up behind her as the little girl put her arms round her mother's neck. She jumped — mostly because of her guilty conscience, upsetting an open bottle of medicine which stood on the desk. She swung round and slapped Sharon across her face.

For a moment neither of them moved, they just stood staring at each other, the child with amazement which gradually turned to fear, Rose with pure horror at what she had done. She'd never laid a hand on Sharon before. Neither she nor Tom believed in that kind of punishment. Then Sharon let out a piercing wail and Rose snatched her up, cuddling her, burying her face in the sweet smelling hair at the nape of her neck.

'Oh, baby, forgive me. I didn't mean it, honestly I didn't. You frightened Mummy. I thought you were a burglar,' she added, hoping the idea might distract the little girl, but she went on crying as though her heart would break, her breath coming in gasps as she tried to speak.

Rose carried her through into the kitchen and sat her at the table. Going to the fridge she got out a tray of ice lollies she made herself and always kept in the freezer section.

'Now love, which one would you like — orange, raspberry . . . '

Sharon turned her head away. 'Don't want one. You smacked me!' There was a faint pink mark across the chubby cheek. It hadn't been a hard slap but Rose felt as if she'd half killed the child.

'Oh, darling, please forgive me. Really I didn't know it was you . . . '

At last the sobbing abated, but not the hiccups, and the child's blue eyes were puffed and red so that Rose felt another stab of guilt. She knew her behaviour since Alex had arrived had been unforgivable, both to Tom and Sharon. She had acted so out of character, and she knew Mary had noticed, although she was far too kind to make any remark — at least to her.

For a moment she caught her breath, wondering if she suspected anything. She'd given Rose some curious looks once or twice lately, and she'd been obviously surprised at the idea of the evening classes. Had Tom been talking to his mother about her? She wondered. Was it so obvious that she was going to meet another man?

At the thought of Alex and the money, she glanced at her watch. She'd have to go into town and get it before the banks closed, and she still hadn't written the cheque.

At last, with the resilience of childhood, Sharon was pacified, she and Huggy were taking a lollie out into the garden, and Rose returned to her attempt at copying Tom's signature.

Eventually she achieved a reasonable likeness, thankful that like most doctors, his writing was hardly legible, and it wasn't too difficult to copy. She took a blank cheque from her book, signed it and then countersigned it. Really it didn't look too bad. But she'd try the

Building Society first, not sure how much was left in the share account. If she had no luck there, then as a last resort she'd take the cheque into the bank.

Sharon was reluctant to leave the garden on such a perfect day.

'Can I go to Gran's?' she pleaded when Rose dressed her to go into town with her, but she dared not face Mary today knowing she was going to see Alex in the evening. She felt sure Tom's mother would see through the guilt written all over her face.

'No, love, Gran's busy. We'll go and feed the swans and ducks on the estuary while we're in Queensbridge. You get a bag and fill it with some stale bread. OK?'

Sharon was a little pacified by this promise and hurried off on her errand. Rose put on blue denim jeans and a matching tee shirt, Alex liked her to be casually dressed, and she wouldn't have much time to change — also as she was ostensibly going to a pottery class, neither Tom nor Marjorie would expect her to be dressed up. How cunning she was getting, she thought ruefully.

When she got to the building society offices and asked for a withdrawal slip, the girl gave her a rather odd glance.

'Mrs Murray, would you wait just a moment, please?' she said, 'the manager would like a word.'

Rose's heart missed a beat. For a moment she looked round for a way of escape, but the girl had already opened the door to the manager's office. She entered as if she were going to the scaffold. The manager was a bright young whizz kid; the type she and Tom had secretly named sharp dressers. He rose to his feet, came round the desk and pulled out a chair for Rose and one for Sharon, who climbed on to it and sat staring at him solemnly.

'The girl said you wanted to see me,' Rose said slowly, unable to bear the silence any longer.

The man balanced his paper knife on one finger — a shiny notice said in black letters his name — Mr E F Letterford . . . It seemed even whizz kids could be embarrassed, she thought, distracted for the moment.

'Mrs Murray, it is rather difficult, what I have to say, but I do hope you will take it in the spirit in which it is meant.' He paused a moment as if seeking the right words, then he said, 'Your husband came to see me the other day. He asked for your share book to be made up to date — of course we do periodic checks on the computer with head office to make sure there is no mistake in our local records . . . ' He paused again and Rose wondered for one desperate moment what he would do if she fainted.

'I'm sorry to say we found there were only two pounds left in the account. I understand you wanted to withdraw a hundred, is that so?'

For a moment Rose couldn't speak, it was as if all the muscles in her throat had become paralysed, at last she managed to say, 'Oh, I see, thank you.'

She got to her feet. 'I . . . we'll have to see what we can do to build it up again. It isn't easy at the moment. Tom's only a country doctor.' She hesitated. 'Anyway it's possible we shall be moving to London soon. He's got the offer of a very good job there.'

Mr Letterford got up, too, thankful the uncomfortable interview was over. He managed a smile which touched his mouth but didn't reach his eyes.

'Quite. We shall be sorry to lose your account here, of course, but we will have it transferred to another of our offices near you as soon as you know what district you will be living in.'

Somehow Rose got out of the building into the hot June sunshine. Sharon looked up at her.

'What did he mean, Mummy? Why wouldn't he let you have any money? How will you do your shopping?'

'I have a little in my purse, love, but we'll go to the bank first.' Her limbs were trembling and she was icy cold in spite of the heat of the sun. What on earth would happen if the teller in the bank realized Tom's signature had been forged? Would they call the police?

She felt physically sick, her palms moist with sweat, but it had to be done. She dare not go and see Alex without taking him some money, and she was pretty certain it was no empty threat he had made that if she didn't, he would contact Tom — or was she telling herself this story because in her heart she had to see Alex again . . . to feel his lips on hers . . .

'Oh God,' she murmured, 'please help me out of this terrible muddle I've got into.'

She felt a moment of bitterness. After all the mess had been none of her seeking — or had it? Of course what she should have done, what any sensible right-minded person would have done would be to have gone to the police at once, to tell David, regardless of whatever consequences it might have had. She should have relied on Tom's love, of the love of all who knew her, to weather such a storm. But now she even wondered if Tom, knowing of her past, would have stuck by her. His words still echoed in her ears, 'Perhaps it would be better if I went to London on my own!'

The bank was busy, for which she was thankful, they wouldn't have so much time to examine the signature.

She pushed the cheque under the plate glass panel that separated her from the girl teller. It was one she knew and she gave Rose a bright smile.

'Isn't it smashing weather? Wish I lived where you do.'

Rose tried to smile back, feeling as if her lips were stretched tightly over her teeth, watching the girl as she glanced at the cheque, and paused a moment, rubber stamp in one hand. Rose closed her eyes. This is it, she thought, but the girl only said, 'Would you like five or ten pound notes, Mrs Murray?'

'I — oh — five I think, thank you.' They weren't quite so easy to trace.

The girl counted out the notes,

pinned the cheque to a piece of paper
on which she scribbled something
— Rose wondered if it was an
instruction to check the signatures, but
now she didn't care. She had the
money, she wouldn't think of the future
— not the distant future.

The pottery class started at seven
o'clock.

She put Sharon to bed. The little girl
seemed uneasy, disturbed and fretful as
if she knew everything was not as it
should be — or perhaps in a way she
still smarted from the slap. Much to
Rose's relief the mark had vanished
— at least from the child's cheek, but
what about her memory . . . she knew
that kind of behaviour could affect a
child for life, especially when it was so
out of character. What on earth would
Tom think if he knew, and how could
she stop Sharon telling him?

She laid the table and put out cold
meat and salad for Tom when he
returned and laid a place for Marjorie.
He was still out on his rounds and she

was thankful at least she wouldn't have to face him before she left.

Marjorie arrived ten minutes late looking flustered.

'I thought I wouldn't be able to come. It was Kim, my dog, he ran out of the gate into the road — some idiot had left it open — and it took me ages to find him. I think there must have been a bitch in an interesting condition in the next street. Sorry I'm late.'

Rose, who had been pacing from the window to the door and back again like a caged tiger, tried to look unconcerned.

'Don't worry, it's awfully kind of you to come anyway, Tom should be in soon and I've left you some food if you'd like it.'

'Thanks.' Marjorie gave her a curious look. 'What are you going to make at this class? Pots, jugs, that kind of thing or is it more sculpture?'

For a moment Rose was taken aback. Of course she hadn't realized she would be expected to come back full of what she had done, even with a sample of her work.

'I don't quite know. I fixed it all up in rather a hurry because it isn't easy to get in.' She didn't dare look at Marjorie who replied slowly.

'Yes, it did seem rather a rush job. Anyway I hope you enjoy it. They say it's very relaxing and therapeutic.'

Rose ran out to her car and drove away swiftly. She would have to put in an appearance at the class and say on this first occasion that she must leave early. Why, oh why, did she have to complicate her life to such an extent that she was lying to everyone? And why put her happy, contented existence in jeopardy just for the sake of an old love? The trouble was the old love was inviting, exciting, different and she was weak, always had been where Alex was concerned. There was something about him, something appealing, irresistible. She supposed it was the elusive thing known as charm, or perhaps just sheer animal sex appeal.

That had been another hurdle she had had to cross; while she was seeing Alex, while she wasn't sure where her heart was leading her, she had had to make an excuse to Tom so she could sleep in the spare room. She couldn't share his bed when she had come straight from Alex's arms. At least I still have that amount of self-respect left, she thought ruefully. She had played with the idea of asking Pat for some sleeping tablets. She had told Tom the reason for her moving was that she was restless, letting him think it was the threat of the new job, but she changed her mind about the tablets and simply lay tossing and turning in the tiny spare room, trying to sort out the tumult inside her.

When she arrived at the college, the class had already started. The tutor looked annoyed at her late arrival.

'I'm awfully sorry, the baby sitter was late.' At least that was true.

He shrugged. 'Well there isn't a wheel free at the moment so you'd better just get the feel of the clay over here.' He led her to a bench and put a lump of wet clay into her hands. At any other time she would have loved the feel of it, the malleable resilience, but now she was too preoccupied, too worried. She wore an old smock which she had used when she was carrying Sharon.

As the tutor turned to go back to the others she said quickly, 'I'm awfully sorry but I'll have to go before the class finishes, it's — ' He cut her off before she finished. 'The baby sitter. You married women, you're all the same. Get bored with the old routine at home. I should have thought you had enough on your hands without cluttering up my pottery class.'

He strode away before she could answer, although what she would have said she didn't know — in some ways he was right. Fortunately he seemed fully preoccupied with the other students who were all young and keen, so after about half an hour she slipped away, washed her hands and took off her smock.

At least if anyone checked she could prove she'd been to the class . . .

14

At last she turned into the rutted lane that led to the forest and as usual, all else but her coming meeting with Alex vanished from her mind.

There was no sign of life at the cottage as she drove up, but she was used to that. He would have heard the car engine and be taking no chances.

She parked the Mini round the back where the stolen car still stood hidden with brushwood. As she got out Alex opened the back door.

'Hi, honey. How's my girl then? Looking as beautiful as ever.' He held out his arms and she went into them, feeling again the old familiar thrill along her nerves as his lips came down on hers.

'Come on then. I've got us a meal, such as it is. Can't do much with the equipment I've got, but I hope it won't be for much longer. Saw a pal of mine in Plymouth the other day, and he's heard on the grapevine about a chance of making some bread, lollie, but I won't bore you with the details.' He grinned at her. 'Got better things to do with our time, haven't we, Rosie?'

For a moment she pulled away from him. 'Does that mean you're going away?'

'Possibly . . . '

She didn't know if she was glad or sorry. 'I shan't be able to bring you any more money, Alex, Tom's getting suspicious. He's checked up at the Building Society.' She dropped her gaze.

'Has he now! Well, I hope you've managed to bring something because otherwise I'm going to be hungry, and you wouldn't want poor old Alex to starve, would you now?' he said with a touch of drama. She felt a moment's impatience with his attitude.

'I don't think that's likely. After all

I've brought you a lot of money and my jewellery.'

'Look, love, I don't want to be rude, but those bits and bobs hardly fetched enough to pay the milk bill. You know what it's like with inflation and everything, a chap can't live decently. Anyway, if you'd come with me you'd have had some jewellery worth hocking.'

She took out her bag. 'Here's another hundred pounds, and that's it, honestly.'

He took it from her, folding it and pushing it carelessly into the back pocket of his jeans. 'Lovely. Thanks, pet.'

For a moment she drew away from him, thinking how lightly he had treated the money which had caused her so much anguish to obtain.

'It was awful, I had to . . . to forge Tom's signature.'

He threw back his head and guffawed with laughter.

'Oh, that's rich, it really is. Forging

your husband's signature for money for your lover . . . greater love hath no woman. You catch on fast, we'll make something out of you yet.'

She turned away from him.

'I don't think it's funny. Tom's worked hard for that money, apart from the fact that I'll probably be sent to prison when they find out.'

'Don't you believe it. They'll tell you not to be a naughty girl and not to do it again and put you on probation for a year.'

It was so close to what had happened before, the thought made her shiver. He took her hand.

'Come on, love. I've opened the wine, eat, drink and be merry — for tomorrow we go on probation.'

She felt a growing irritation. Somehow things weren't turning out as she had been anticipating.

He drew her down on to the bed beside him.

'Got a couple of lovely trout. I thought I'd fry them. Fancy that, do

177

you?' He stroked the hair back from her forehead. 'Lovely hair, shining and free, like corn silk. I was always proud of it when you were my girl. Thank God you've had the sense not to have it cut . . . ' He broke off suddenly, jumping to his feet, spilling his glass of wine.

'What the hell's that?'

'I didn't hear anything.'

'An engine — could be a 'copter, but more likely a car, and coming up the track.'

He swung round. 'You weren't followed by any chance were you?' his eyes narrowed.

'Of course not. How could I be? I'd been in Queensbridge to the pottery class, and come straight here after. No one would be likely to follow me. Why should they?'

Without saying any more he went over to where his jacket hung on a hook behind the front door and took a revolver from the pocket, checking the loading in the chamber, clicking off the safety catch.

Rose got to her feet, her heart pounding.

'What are you going to do? Where did you get that gun from?'

'One question at a time, my lovely. I never travel anywhere without a gun. 'Tisn't safe with all the villains there are about these days, and I'm about to defend myself if some nosey parker has come looking for me.'

Keeping out of sight, he looked through the small window which gave on to the track.

'What sort of car does your old man drive?' he asked slowly.

Without answering she came over and stood beside him.

Tom's car was coming slowly along the track.

Quick as a flash, Alex swung round, the back of his hand slapping Rose across the mouth so that she felt the blood start where her teeth had been driven into the soft flesh.

'You bitch! You told him! You grassed

on me. Well, you won't get away with it and neither will he.'

Grasping her roughly by the shoulder he dragged her in front of him by the window. He held her hands behind her, locked in a grip from which she knew she couldn't escape, the gun in his other hand.

'Right,' he said through clenched teeth, 'I'll show Doctor Bloody Murray I mean business. I'll shut his mouth so he can't squeak at least.'

Rose opened her mouth to try to warn Tom, she squirmed and wriggled in Alex's grasp, but it was hopeless, no sound came out and his vice-like grip increased.

She watched, mesmerized, as Tom stopped the car in front of the cottage. He sat for a moment staring at it as if he wasn't sure if he had come to the right place.

Please God, let him go away, she prayed silently. I don't mind what happens to me; don't let anything bad happen to Tom.

As if reading her thoughts, Alex said, 'If he's got any sense he'll scarper, and if you so much as make a sound you'll get this right in one side and out the other.' She felt the hard cold barrel of the gun in the small of her back.

Tom had evidently decided at last to investigate and got out of the car, leaving the door open. As he came towards the cottage Alex smashed the glass of the window with the butt of the revolver. Tom stopped dead.

'No further, amigo,' Alex shouted, 'or I'll blow your little wifey to smith-ereens.' Tom glanced at the window and saw Rose with Alex behind her.

'Don't be an idiot,' he said slowly. 'Whoever you are you know you can't win that way. It's stupid to add murder to whatever you've already done that you're on the run for.'

'Please, Tom, go away.' At last Rose managed to call out in her anguish.

As if he hadn't heard her he said, 'I'll give you just two minutes to come out with your hands up and your gun on

181

the grass here, whatever your name is, after that I'm coming in.'

'You must be joking. It's the one with the gun holds the whip hand, remember.'

Rose was certain she would faint, her knees sagged, but Alex pushed her against the window frame, the gun still in her back.

'It's up to you, squire. Depends on how much you value your wife staying alive.'

Rose shut her eyes. She was certain she was about to die, and now she found that all she cared was that Tom shouldn't be hurt . . .

'Go on,' she said softly, 'kill me, it would be one solution anyway.' As she spoke she felt Alex move his arm, then there was a terrific explosion which nearly blew her off her feet. She opened her eyes as a flash almost blinded her. But it wasn't she who had been hit. As she watched, Tom staggered and fell forward. Wrenching herself free she ran towards the door, sobbing, tripping over a loose board as she did so, not caring whether Alex shot her or not . . .

'You've killed him! You've killed him,' she shouted, as she struggled with the latch on the door.

At that moment she heard another shot from behind and momentarily thrown off balance, she swung round.

David stood framed in the open doorway behind her, a smoking gun in his hand. Alex sat on the floor, clutching his leg which was bleeding.

'Filthy pig!' he yelled at David who had picked up the revolver where he had dropped it.

'I'll deal with you in a moment,' David said and turning to Rose, 'You OK, love?'

She nodded. 'I'm all right — he shot Tom.' She'd got the door open now and ran to where Tom was sitting up, trying to get to his feet.

'Tom, darling . . . '

His face was pale as death, but he grinned and said, 'Are you OK?'

'Thank God. I thought you were

dead.' And she burst into tears.

'Takes more than that to kill a Murray. He got me in the knee cap and I hit my head going down.' He rubbed a lump on his forehead. 'If you could just help me to the car I've got my bag in there. It's a case of physician, heal thyself! I think it's only a flesh wound.'

He put one arm along her shoulders and with her help he managed to half hop, half limp to the car.

'Is old Dave OK? I heard another shot. That fellow in there must be a nutter.'

'He shot Alex in the leg.'

'Alex?' He looked at her. 'You did know this chap then?'

She looked away, unable for the moment to meet his candid gaze, or explain.

'Yes. I've got an awful lot to tell you, to explain, but I think it'll have to do later . . . all I want is to get home. But how did you know where I was?'

'I had to make a call in Queensbridge and I thought I'd call at the college and take you for a drink at the end of your class.' He paused, and looked a little sheepish. 'You were just driving away and when I saw you were taking the road away from Swallowdene, I followed you. I was sure you were in some kind of trouble — danger even. I've thought for some time — known, I suppose, really — that something was wrong, more than just unhappiness over the job. You don't come as close to someone as I have to you without at least noticing their moods, their feelings.'

He winced a little as she tightened the dressing she had put on his leg.

'So I went to have a talk with Dave.'

Her blood froze. Did that mean David had told him about her past? Not that it mattered all that much. It would have to come out now, but she would rather be the one to tell him, to try to seek his forgiveness.

'Actually David took a more serious view of the whole thing than I did, professional acumen, I suppose. Anyway he seemed to have a theory that you were being blackmailed when I told him about the money situation.'

She looked away and said in a whisper, 'I know. I'm so desperately sorry. I don't honestly know what came over me.'

'Well, this isn't the time to talk about it, as long as you're OK.' He squeezed her hand, then he said slowly, 'I was more surprised than anything, not at you, but at myself, how little I really knew you who I love so much, am married to, live with. Then I began to wonder if it was something that had happened before we met, something that had affected you, but I couldn't understand why it should suddenly have done so. I suppose that only confirms the point that none of us knows another completely — ever.'

At his words Rose was more than ever overcome with shame and remorse for the way she had behaved, but this was not the place, or the time, to talk of it or to tell Tom she loved him — that at least she knew now, when she had thought he was seriously wounded or dead, all she had wanted was to die herself. Alex being wounded had affected her not at all.

'We must get you to hospital to have that knee looked at,' she said, and he laughed.

'OK, Doctor, whatever you say. The roles reversed, eh? I'm the patient and you the physician.'

David had fixed handcuffs on Alex and was helping him to the police car.

'You OK, Tom?'

Tom nodded, jerking his head towards Alex. 'What about him?'

'Only a flesh wound, but it'll stop his little capers for a bit. I think, if you can manage it, you'd better come back to the station and make a statement.' He paused. 'Rose can drive you and I'll send someone out to collect her car, and the stolen one, later on.'

Rose concentrated on the road, trying not to shake Tom up more than she could help. She never liked driving with him in the car for he was a first class driver himself and tended to be over-sensitive to anyone else, but now he lay back with his eyes closed; she glanced at him once or twice, longing in a way to talk to him, to try to explain, if she ever could, but it had to wait.

'I knew Alex years ago when we lived in London. I wasn't much more than a kid,' was all she said.

He didn't open his eyes, but replied, 'I don't think I really want to know, Rose. Not at the moment anyway.'

The X-ray at the hospital proved that Tom's kneecap had been cracked by the bullet, but it had passed through and out the other side so should cause no lasting damage. They insisted on keeping him in hospital for a few days, however, to make sure everything was in order and that he rested the leg.

'Look, old boy,' the young houseman said, much to Tom's secret amusement, 'be sensible. You know what you'd tell one of your patients in the same circumstances, and it may make all the difference between having a limp for the rest of your life or being able to walk normally. You know that as well as I do.'

Reluctantly, Tom was persuaded to stay for a small operation to be done. The next morning Rose went to see him, knowing that she had to explain to him everything that had happened, about Alex, and she had decided that if he felt he wanted his freedom after he had heard, then of course she would give it to him. She had lain awake all night trying to make up her mind, to reach a decision, for having to live without him now she knew would break her heart, but she owed it to him. She realized only too well where her real love lay. How could she, even for a moment, have doubted that dear, steady, loving Tom was the man for her. Alex had been a brief flame that had attracted her like a moth to a candle, a passion that flared up and died like a burned out match. Now she bitterly regretted what she had done and would have given everything she had to be able to go back to that June day when he had first rung her up.

She had brought some roses from the garden, Tom's favourite, Prima Ballerina, with the glorious perfume which filled the little side ward where he had been put. The chief nursing officer had grinned when he said the general ward was good enough for him.

'Maybe it is, but we should have the other patients coming to you for advice. They all know you're a doctor, added to which somehow it seems to give a bad image to the profession if a doctor is ill. People think you are invulnerable, have a kind of immunity to disease.'

Tom had given in; he was too tired and now too shocked at what had happened, to argue.

Rose stood at the bottom of the bed.

'How are you feeling?' It was almost like talking to a stranger because she had no idea what his feelings were now.

He smiled. She made a beautiful picture in her blue linen dress, her hair tied back, the only make up a touch of coral lipstick. She reminded him of a repentant child who has been punished, except that under her eyes were deep purple shadows as if a finger had smudged them there and he guessed she hadn't had much sleep. He longed to take her in his arms, although he was still puzzled. David had told him about Alex, the bank raid years ago and his fleeing to South America, but none of it made sense or tied up with Rose. He patted the bed.

'Come and sit down.'

'I'll just put these in water . . . ' She was trying to delay the moment when she had to tell him.

She came back with the vase and put it on the locker by his bed, standing by it with her hands clasped in front of her.

'Tom I have to tell you something . . . '

He took her hand, placing it between both of his, a habit he had always had and now it brought tears sharply to her eyes with the sweet familiarity of the gesture, yet she couldn't draw away.

'I know, love, but I won't eat you . . . '

She couldn't smile or she would have burst into tears. 'You see, Alex and I . . . oh, it's all so long ago, like another world, but it has to be told. I got involved with him and this gang. I had no idea what they were planning, I know that sounds ridiculously naïve, but I was only seventeen and had led a terribly sheltered life. My mother and father were in their forties when I was born and it was more like being brought up by grandparents. Of course when it all came out I think they nearly died, that's why we came to Devon, away from where it all happened, all their friends. Alex had run off to South America. I thought I'd never see him again, I didn't want to, I'd almost forgotten him, and then . . . ' a sob broke from her. He pulled her down towards him.

'And then like a bad dream he turned

192

up to haunt you out of the past. My poor darling, why didn't you tell me? Don't you know I love you? Love isn't just for the good times, it's even more for the bad ones, wouldn't you have stood by me if the situation had been reversed?'

As she looked at him her love was so strong, so intense it felt almost suffocating as she said softly. 'Of course.'

'Then let's forget it ever happened, forget Alex and everything to do with him. Anything that is dreadful, when it is brought out into the open, ceases to be so awful, doesn't it?'

'A haunting from the past,' she murmured. 'Yes, of course, that's an exact description of what it was.'

'It's strange,' he went on, 'have you noticed how Shakespeare always has the right words for any situation? Do you remember from 'As You Like It', 'If thou remember's not the slightest folly That ever love did make thee run into, Thou hast not lov'd ... we that are true lovers run into strange capers.'' He drew her down to him and she felt the warm haven of his arms as his lips found hers.

THE END